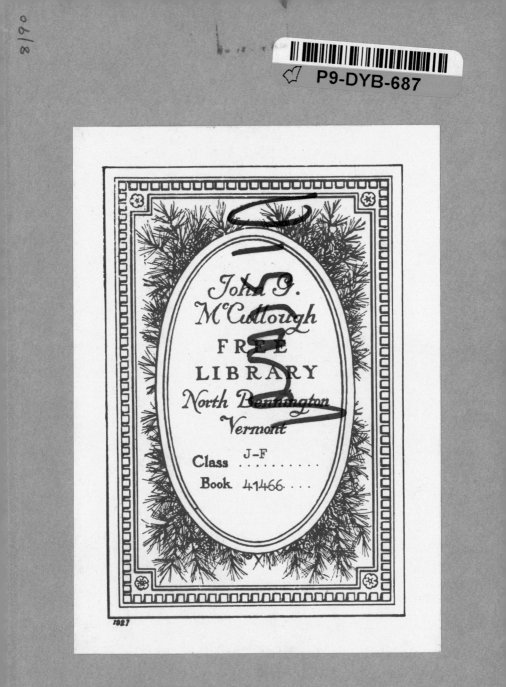

# Secrets of a
# Summer Spy

# Secrets of a Summer Spy

## By Janice Jones

Bradbury Press
New York

Bradbury Press
An Affiliate of Macmillan, Inc.
866 Third Avenue, New York, NY 10022
Collier Macmillan Canada, Inc.

Printed and bound in the United States of America
First Edition
10   9   8   7   6   5   4   3   2   1

The text of this book is set in Bodoni Book
Map by Ralph Jones

*Library of Congress Cataloging-in-Publication Data*

Jones, Janice.
    Secrets of a summer spy / by Janice Jones. — 1st American ed.
        p.    cm.
    Summary: Thirteen-year-old Ronnie, part of a trio of best friends that seems to be falling apart because Amy and Jimmy are growing up faster than she is, finds solace in the company of her island's eccentric catlady, an eighty-three-year-old retired concert pianist.
    ISBN 0-02-747861-0
    [1. Friendship—Fiction.   2. Old age—Fiction.   3. Islands—Fiction.]   I. Title.
PZ7.J7202Se   1990
[Fic]—dc20        89-38156   CIP   AC

*For my daughter,*
*Rachel Anne*

Special thanks to my family, for their encouragement and loving support; Jim Murphy, for his time and suggestions; Sharon Steinhoff, for her insightful editing; and Louise Stinetorf, for her example and friendship.

"Standing with reluctant feet,
Where the brook and river meet,
Womanhood and childhood fleet!"

*Henry Wadsworth Longfellow*

# CONTENTS

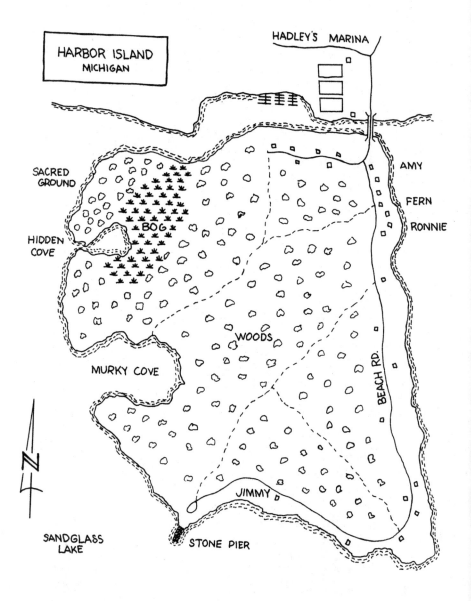

# 1

# Amy's Return

*O*ld *lady Peet leaned over her back porch* railing, parted the branches of the shrubbery directly above my head, and stared down at me.

"Stand up now, young lady. You can't sit out here in the bushes all night."

The juniper scratched my face as I straightened up, feeling very embarrassed at having been caught in the act of spying. "I'm sorry about running over your cat with my bike the other day," I stammered. "It was an accident, honest."

"Well, come inside and tell that to Tomcat," replied Mrs. Peet.

"I'd better not," I said, untangling my legs from the shrub. "It's late and I've got to get home."

"That may be," the old woman said, her voice stern. "But it would be very impolite not to apologize to Tomcat, now wouldn't it?" She opened the screen door and motioned me inside.

My stomach did a flip-flop, and I stood rooted to the spot, unable to make up my mind. Should I go in or take off running? Then I remembered how Jimmy said I was the bravest girl he knew. And how Amy had tricked him into walking her home, leaving me standing alone on the beach. Amy would never be daring enough to go into the old catlady's house, I reasoned. Here was my chance to impress Jimmy, and I was going to take it. I stepped up on the porch and walked past Mrs. Peet into the kitchen.

Amy Parrish, Jimmy Jackman, and I had spent our summers together on Harbor Island for as long as we could remember. Jimmy and I lived on the island year-round, but Amy and her parents only came to northern Michigan when school was out. The Parrishes lived four hours away by car in Detroit, where Amy's parents taught school. Mr. Parrish loved to fish, and Amy's mom liked to sketch by the lake, so a summer cottage on Harbor Island kept everyone happy.

All I could think about the last week of eighth grade

2

was Amy's return. Nothing had prepared me for how much she had changed.

The day she arrived, we agreed to meet Jimmy at the rock and gravel pier, just like old times. When we were younger, Amy had said we three were "as close as clams," and we had called ourselves the Clamdiggers ever since. Each summer, we toasted the group with a special ceremony at the pier.

Standing on the tip of the old stone pier, surrounded by miles and miles of choppy water, was like standing on the end of the world. The air tasted like wet sand, and the sharp breeze stung your face as it whipped in off the lake. If you looked to the west, you could see where Sandglass ended at the town of Northwood, with the Lutheran church tower sticking up above the trees. Looking straight across the water to the opposite shoreline, you could see a few blurry white dots that close up became the elaborate, Victorian-style cottages of Mallard's Landing—a resort for rich summer people. To the east, Sandglass looked endless, just like the ocean. Actually it ran on for ten miles or so to where it ended in the Pere Marquette State Forest.

Amy and I were already at the tip of the pier when Jimmy showed up. He took a long, sideways glance at Amy and climbed the big, flat boulder that jutted out over the water. When he turned to look down on us, the breeze blew his shaggy blond hair into his eyes, and I sensed trouble.

"Welcome back," he said, offering Amy his arm.

"Thanks," she said, taking it and winking at me.

I put my hand out, too, but Jimmy didn't notice. He was busy looking at Amy's hairstyle. She had permed her dark brown, almost black hair into wispy bangs and shoulder-length curls that framed her face and made her light violet eyes seem bigger. Jimmy also stole a fast glance at the front of her rib-knit shirt, then turned away quickly to face the lake. I could see the back of his ears turning red. Amy used to be flat like me, but she had come back from Detroit with definite boobs. Jimmy wasn't used to her new look, and neither was I.

"Hey, how about me?" I said, tugging on the canvas strap that dangled from the flap of Jimmy's backpack.

"Yeah, Ronnie, come on." He never looked at me—I guessed his face was still red.

I scrambled up the rock to stand next to them, and we watched several boats racing back and forth in the distance, in spite of the whitecaps.

"It's too bad we have to wait till Tuesday to get the *Amy Mae* out on the lake," Jimmy said. Amy's dad had bought a new boat and named it the *Amy Mae* after Amy and her mother, whose first name was Mae. We wanted to try it out right away, but it was the Friday of Memorial Day weekend, and we weren't allowed on the lake by ourselves on holidays because of all the tourists.

4

"Let's get started with the toast," Amy said.

"Wait! We can't forget the clams," I reminded her. I sat on the boulder and dangled my legs until my feet found the tops of some half-submerged, mossy rocks at the water's edge. A wave washed over the toes of my running shoes as I bent down, twisted around, and crawled into a small opening under the base of the boulder. It had taken us an entire summer, many years ago, to dig out enough rocks and gravel to make a cave big enough for a secret meeting place. Once inside, I found the three special necklaces of clam shells lying near the back wall.

"Whew! These are gross!" Amy said after I climbed back up and handed her one.

"Aw, quit complaining and put it on," I insisted.

"Don't you think we're getting a little old for this stuff?" she asked. Amy and I were both thirteen, but Jimmy was fourteen and a half—almost a sophomore.

"You're right," Jimmy agreed. He gave her that crooked smile of his that shows all his teeth down one side. "But it just wouldn't be tradition without it."

Amy made a face as she held the rotting strings in her nail tips and carefully put the necklace over her head. A wave crashed against the pier and sent up a fine spray that wet our legs.

"Hurry up," I said, wishing I had brought a jacket. "It's cold out here."

Jimmy opened the pop he'd packed in his knapsack

5

and handed a can to Amy and one to me. We held them out to the lake and chanted together, "Oh Sandglass Lake, mother of the loons and fishes, we swear by the shells we wear that we are as close as clams, and nothing will ever come between us."

"Clamdiggers forever!" Jimmy shouted.

"Here, here," I said. We rattled our shells and took a drink from our cans.

"I feel silly." Amy pouted.

I didn't think it was silly. It was supposed to be a solemn vow—a tradition that we had kept for years.

I handed Amy my grape fizz. She passed her Diet Pepsi to Jimmy, and he gave me his root beer. We drank, switched cans, and drank again.

"Now for the best part," Jimmy said. We carefully climbed down onto the slippery, wave-washed rocks at the mouth of the cave and let some of the lake water run into our cans. We clicked them together and drank. Lake water tastes terrible, but it's not so bad mixed with pop. Jimmy swallowed his in loud gulps. I took a small sip. Amy raised her can to her mouth, but I think she faked it.

We crawled into our cave, and Jimmy built a fire in the pit near the opening. From his knapsack, he took out the marshmallows and chocolate chip cookies. We sharpened the ends of some sticks with Jimmy's pocketknife, roasted the marshmallows, and smeared them on the cookies.

6

"It's cold in here, too," I said, rubbing my arms.

"Here," Jimmy offered, putting his arm around me. It was hard and knotty from a winter of basketball, and it felt warm against my skin. I watched Amy eat a marshmallow, careful not to let any stick to her lips, and snuggle closer to Jimmy.

"I'm cold, too," she complained, dropping her head and rolling her eyes up at him. He took the last bite of his marsh-cookie and draped his other arm around her. Then we sat, stinking of old clam shells and gazing at the long moss strands that swayed around the rocks at the mouth of the cave.

Suddenly Jimmy's hand moved a little. It stopped under my arm, so the ends of his fingers reached the edge of my breast, or where it would have been if I weren't so flat. He coughed and squirmed, like he was settling in against the hard rock, and his fingers inched forward a bit more. What was going on here? I wondered. Jimmy and I had been friends forever, and he'd never tried anything like this before. I looked over at Amy. She was wiggling around, smiling stupidly at Jimmy.

*Whoomph!* Eighty pounds of wet, yellow dog landed in our laps.

"Boogie, get off," I said, pushing at his rump.

"P.U.!" Amy said, holding her nose. "That dog has the worst fish breath in the state of Michigan."

"Aw, Boogers doesn't smell any worse than your

necklace," Jimmy said, taking his arms from around Amy and me. Jimmy had always called Boogie "Boogers" when he was a puppy, and the nickname still seemed to fit.

"He must have been out catching lunch," I suggested. Boogie was always too fat, and Jimmy had him on a never-ending diet. Instead of losing weight, though, Boogie had learned to hunt and fish, and he stayed as round as ever.

We were all trying to push Jimmy's dog out of the cave when we heard a faint sound that could have been a car horn. Harbor Island was small enough that whenever our parents wanted us, they just went out to the car and honked. We each had our own code. Jimmy hurried out of the cave to listen. "One long and two short. It's for me," he said.

"I'd better get home, too," Amy sighed. "I have all my unpacking to do." Amy and I took off our necklaces and handed them down to Jimmy, who had returned to the cave to put out the fire. Then we all ran along the pier, kicking loose gravel into the lake, until we were back to the shore. We'd left our bikes there, at the turnaround loop where Beach Road dead-ended.

"Good to have you back, Amy." Jimmy waved. "See ya." He hopped on his bike and pedaled off toward his house, with Boogie trotting behind him. Jimmy lived a short distance from the pier, in the last cottage on

Beach Road—Harbor Island's only road. But Amy and I lived near the bridge to the mainland, at the other end of Beach Road, so we took the shortcut through the woods.

I rode behind Amy on the narrow path, and our bike tires made ruts in the soft dirt. The greenish white flowers of the Solomon's seal arched over the edges of the trail.

Harbor Island is really a peninsula about a mile and a half long that is separated from the mainland by a man-made channel. A short, wooden plank bridge is the only way in or out. We all knew the story about how, after the first twenty-some cottages had been built along the eastern shore, some rich man had bought up the rest of the island. For the last twenty years the land had sat undeveloped, mostly woods and wetland. My dad said that someday the woods would probably be chopped up into tiny lots and the bog would be drained for a golf course, just like across the lake at Mallard's Landing. I hoped that would never happen.

"You know," Amy said over her shoulder. "I think Jim likes me."

"Of course he likes you," I agreed. "Why are you calling him 'Jim' all of a sudden?"

"Why not? 'Jimmy' sounds so childish, don't you think?"

"I never thought about it," I said.

9

"He's changed. He's taller, his hair's grown out wavy, and his eyes—they're sooo bluuue. He looks at least fifteen, maybe even sixteen—and he likes me."

I thought Jimmy's eyes weren't any bluer than before, and his hair needed cutting. "What do you mean, he likes you?"

She rode slower and lowered her voice. "Back there, in the cave, when Jim had his arm around me, he . . . well, he . . . tried to feel around," she confided.

So I was right, I thought. But that didn't seem like Jimmy. During the school year we rode the bus into Northwood together every day (along with the second-grade Kowalski twins and Jimmy's older sister, Margo). He was just like a big brother to me. Still, the girls at school were always whispering in the bathroom about older boys trying stuff like that. And I hadn't seen as much of Jimmy over the winter, with him being in high school and on the basketball team. I was about to tell Amy that he had been feeling around with me, too, when she stopped so fast I ran my bike into her rear tire. She held her hand up.

"What are you—"

"Shhh," she whispered. I squeezed my bike up next to hers. "There's someone walking on the trail, up ahead."

"So what? Let's go," I said.

"I think it's the old catlady. I just caught a glimpse

of her through the trees. She's going the same way we are. Maybe we should hang back awhile."

Old lady Peet lived two houses down the road from me, but she kept to herself so we hardly ever saw her. We knew little about her except that she kept a band of half-wild cats, who roamed the island making nuisances of themselves. And sometimes she played scales on a piano. Once in a while, when we passed her house, we heard a series of slow, deliberate notes. My mom called old lady Peet eccentric. Mr. Jackman, Jimmy's dad, once said, "Mrs. Peet is not playing with a full deck."

Another series of car horn blasts echoed through the trees. Three short, pause, three short.

"I can't just sit here," I said. "Mom's honking me in for dinner. I'll bet we can ride right up behind Mrs. Peet and whiz past her before she sees us coming."

"Well . . . maybe," Amy said.

"Get moving," I ordered.

We rode around the bend and saw no one. Pedaling faster, we rounded the next bend, and there she was, a small woman in a print dress walking slowly away from us, a shiny pail in her hand. Amy and I were really sailing along now, and with the trail so narrow, I didn't see how we could get around Mrs. Peet without running her down. Amy saw the problem, too.

"Excuse us," she called out when she was almost on top of the woman, but Mrs. Peet was already stepping aside as though she had heard us coming all along. Amy shot past her, but as I went by I looked down into her pail. It was half-full of tiny strawberries, the kind that grew wild near the cove. If I hadn't been so curious, I might have seen the cat that was next to the old woman's feet. I hardly felt the bump in my tire when I ran over its tail.

# 2

# Prize Catch

*R*aaawwwwahhh!" *the cat screamed, and* jumped up the old woman's dress. Mrs. Peet grabbed for the animal, her pail flying in the air. Strawberries rained on my head as I stood on my bike pedals and pumped hard.

"Cruel child!" she yelled after me.

"Sorry," I yelled back. Amy was almost out of sight, and the bumpy trail rattled my fenders as I chased after her. Neither of us slowed down until we reached the road near my house, where we jumped off our bikes to rest.

"What was that awful scream?" Amy asked.

I looked down into my bike basket, picked out a

strawberry, and threw it in the ditch. "It was the cat," I said softly. "I ran over his tail."

"His tail?" Amy stared at me with a serious face. "Why that's . . . er . . . that's the funniest thing I've ever heard!" She burst into laughter.

I didn't think it was funny at all. What if I had really hurt the cat? I wondered. What if Mrs. Peet yelled at my parents or something?

"Just wait till I tell Jim that you ran down old lady Peet and tried to cut off her cat's tail," Amy said. She hunched over her handlebars and tried to catch her breath.

"Do you think we should go back?" I asked her. "I mean, what if I really broke his tail or something? Maybe old lady Peet needs help."

Amy straightened up and looked at me. "You want to go back? If it was anyone else, I'd go with you. But who knows what the old catlady might do?"

I didn't know, and I didn't want to find out. Not by myself. So we got back on our bikes and rode the rest of the way to my house. As we pulled into the gravel driveway, Amy giggled.

"I didn't think it's *that* funny," I said.

"Oh, yes it is. It's hysterical!"

Ignoring her, I put my bike in the garage. I could hear her snickering as she rode away.

\* \* \*

Early the next morning, Amy came to my house so we could make peanut butter sandwiches and bake a batch of brownies to take fishing. I put raisins in the brownies because Jimmy liked them that way. The hum of distant boat engines through the open kitchen windows was a reminder that the holiday weekend was in full swing. For the next three days, Sandglass Lake would be swarmed by the summer people from Mallard's Landing, the campers from the state parks, and the weekend boaters from Northwood.

While Amy and I got our food ready, Mom and Dad sat at the table drinking coffee and sharing a single piece of toast. Both were dressed for work, Mom in a pale cotton blouse and white slacks, and Dad in his khaki Lake Patrol uniform. My father is a Northwood deputy sheriff, but in the summer he trades in his police car for a sleek patrol cruiser with twin outboard engines and spends his time rescuing stranded boaters, arresting drunken fishermen, and enforcing lake regulations.

Mom gulped the last bite of her toast, went to the sink to rinse her cup, then turned and gave Amy a quick hug. "It's so nice to have you back, Amy. You've certainly grown up into a pretty young lady."

"Thanks, Mrs. Windslow. It's good to be back, even though there isn't much to do here."

What was she talking about, I wondered. No place

on earth could be more exciting than Harbor Island in the summer. There was crawdad hunting, fishing, swimming, boating, waterskiing, spying, and well, the list was endless.

Mom grabbed her white smock and purse off the hook by the door. "Ronnie, would you make sure you're here around four o'clock to put the chicken in?"

"Sure," I answered as she walked out the door. Mom didn't usually work on Saturdays, but the other hygienist at the Northwood Dental Clinic was on vacation.

Dad flipped on the police scanner and listened while he finished his coffee. "Sounds like there's a lot going on. I'd better get out on the lake," he said. On the way out the door he blew me a kiss. "Have fun fishing and catch me a big mess of crappies."

As soon as he was gone, Amy put down the peanut butter knife and pulled the hem of her flowered blouse away from the jelly jar. "Why don't you wear your bathing suit, Ronnie? I've got mine on underneath."

"We're going fishing, not swimming," I said.

"I know," she answered, "but we can still work on our tans." Amy always turned a fantastic shade of brown without trying, but not me. With my fair skin and auburn hair, a bottle of sunscreen lived in the hip pocket of my cutoffs all summer.

"You two ready?" Jimmy called from the other side of the screen door.

16

"All set," I said, grabbing a couple of extra brownies to eat on the way. Jimmy took one out of my hand and bit into it. "Mmmmmm. You remembered the raisins."

I offered one to Amy but she shook her head. "Chocolate's too fattening and it gives me zits."

We grabbed our gear and walked side by side down Beach Road, past Smitty's cottage. We had to split up in front of Mrs. Peet's house to go around a fat black and white cat that was sound asleep in the middle of the road. Everyone on the island hated that cat, because it took at least ten blasts of a car horn to wake it up and get it moving.

"Someday that blimp is going to get it. Kersplat!" Jimmy said, slapping his hands together.

Across the road from the catlady's house, we took the trail that led to Murky Cove and the best crappie fishing on the island. We walked a half mile through thick woods, and then followed the path as it snaked its way around the edge of the big bog.

"I wish I knew what that patch of woods on the other side of the bog was like," I said.

"You always want to know everything," Amy pointed out. "Last time we tried going through that bog, I got stuck in the muck up to my waist. It's lucky it wasn't quicksand."

"Aw, it wasn't as bad as that," Jimmy said.

"Well, how about the time we tried to go by boat?"

Amy reminded us. "The oars kept getting tangled up in the water lilies and the stumps scraped up the dinghy so bad, we had to repaint the whole thing."

"Yeah, my dad was mad about the boat," Jimmy said. "But still . . . there's got to be a way."

I knew every twist of every trail on Harbor Island—where the trillium and lady's slipper grew, and where to find the longest cattail reeds for weaving into placemats. I knew everything, except the secrets that waited in the woods beyond the bog.

"This summer, Jimmy," I said, "we'll get there for sure."

The woods dead-ended at a grassy bank where the lake began. The water was calm in Murky Cove, except for the occasional series of waves that washed in—the wakes from the boats pulling skiers in the distance. Jimmy and I baited our hooks and swung our lines out over the fringe of cattails growing along the shore. Amy sat down on a beach towel and took off her shirt to catch the rays. Her new lavender two-piece was almost small enough to be a bikini.

Jimmy and I fished for over an hour without a nibble. He took turns watching his bobber and stealing glances at Amy's middle.

"Aren't you going to fish?" I asked Amy. I held my pole in one hand and played with the unraveled edge of my worn cutoff's with the other.

"Yeah, I guess." She picked up the worm bucket

and looked inside. Handing it to Jimmy, she smiled and said, "Will you bait my hook for me, Jim?"

Since when couldn't she do it herself? I wondered. I waited for Jimmy to tease her. He always said that if you couldn't handle your own worm, you had no business fishing in the first place.

"Sure," was his answer. He took the bucket, pulled out a night crawler, and threaded it on her hook. He wiped his hands on the front of his jeans above the holey knees, and tossed his head to throw back the stray curl that always hung down over his face.

"Thanks, Jim. Worms are so squirmy-icky," Amy said. As soon as she plopped her line into the water, her cork began to bob. She sat up straight, waiting for the fish to run with it, and the cork went under. Standing, Amy pulled hard, her cane pole bending into a half circle, and lifted a large crappie to the surface. The fish skipped in and out of the water as she dragged it through the cattails toward shore.

"Wow, what luck," Jimmy exclaimed.

Amy gave the pole a final heave and dropped the fish by Jimmy's feet, where it flipped and flopped around, coating itself with sand. "Will you get it off the hook for me, Jim?" she asked, holding the line in her fingers. "Pretty please?"

"Natch," Jimmy said. "Watch this for me, will you, Ronnie?" He handed me his pole, grabbed the fish, unhooked it, and put it on Amy's stringer.

I watched my cork. Instead of bobbing a couple of times first, it went under and stayed there. Holding Jimmy's pole, I jerked on mine, one-handed. Something pulled back, harder than I expected. "Jimmy, take your pole. I've got a big one," I yelled, but Jimmy was bent over the water's edge, tying Amy's stringer.

I dropped Jimmy's pole as the fish ran with my line. "Get the net," I called to Amy. She picked it up and tried to hand it to me.

"No, you use it," I said. "I need both hands for this baby." Pulling the fish toward shore, I'd gotten a glimpse of him: a largemouth bass, a huge one. I had him in the cattails when my line got tangled up with Jimmy's. The fish splashed wildly in the shallow water.

"Wow, it's gigantic!" Jimmy was really excited. "Hold on, Ronnie!" He grabbed his pole and jerked it around, trying to free up my line.

"Well, net him!" I screamed at Amy. "Hurry up!"

She stood on the bank and daintily dipped the net in the water. It was clear she wasn't about to get her feet wet.

I yanked on my pole again and the line tangled tighter around the weeds. The biggest fish I'd ever hooked thrashed and jumped, threatening to get away any second, so I dropped my pole, jumped in the water with my shoes on, and grabbed the line. Jerking it free, I swung the fish to shore. It made a loud smack as it hit Amy right across her bare middle. She squealed and fell backwards into a sit. She deserved that, I thought. Jimmy saved her by grabbing the fish out of her lap. He held it up, his thumb disappearing into its saucer mouth.

"What a keeper! That's the biggest bass we've ever caught!"

"I ever caught," I corrected him.

"Gross, oh gross, fish slime," Amy said, wiping her tummy with her beach towel.

"It won't hurt you," I said, laughing. I expected Jimmy to laugh, too, but instead, he handed me the bass and went over to Amy.

"You okay?" he asked.

Ignoring him, Amy glared in my direction. "You did that on purpose, Veronica Windslow!" She threw her towel on the ground and stomped over to me, hands on hips.

I put one hand on my hip, still holding my fish in the other, and glared back at her. "I did not, Amy Parrish. If you had used the net when I told you, I wouldn't have almost lost my bass."

"Says you!" she shouted, her nose almost touching mine.

Jimmy came up behind her and put his hand on her arm. "Ronnie couldn't see where that fish was going to land, Amy."

"Well, maybe," she conceded, but she didn't sound convinced.

"I've had enough fishing for one day," I said, stepping back and holding my bass high. Its greenish scales glistened in the sun. "I want to get over to Hadley's and weigh this baby. He's going to be this year's entry in the fishing contest." Hadley's Marina was on the mainland, just across the bridge. Every summer, Mr. Hadley sponsored a prize for the biggest bass, and I had just caught the granddaddy of them all. I was going to get my picture in the *Northwood Express* and a new graphite fly rod.

"Yeah," Jimmy agreed, straightening out his line. "I can't wait to see how much it weighs. Twelve pounds, maybe thirteen. I'll bet it's a record."

"What about our picnic lunch?" Amy asked.

"We can eat at Hadley's," Jimmy answered. "Let's go."

Amy and Jimmy walked along the trail a few yards in front of me. My tennies were so wet and muddy that they squished as I followed them, but it didn't matter. Nothing did. The sun made leafy patterns on the trail, the woods were full of birdsong, and I was going to win the fishing contest for sure. When they reached Beach Road by the catlady's house, Amy leaned close to Jimmy and whispered something in his ear. Immediately they stopped walking.

"What's all this secret stuff?" I asked, catching up. They were looking across the road toward Mrs. Peet's.

"I dare you to climb up there and touch one of those cats," Amy said to me.

Up on old lady Peet's roof was an orange tabby cat, head and tail up, and front paw held out as if it were slinking along the gutter. At first you thought it was real, but it never moved. There were two others: a gray cat climbing the rose trellis, and a black one that stood on the little peaked roof over the front door.

I turned to her and asked, "Why don't you, Amy? It was your idea."

"Ronnie's afraid of old lady Peet because she ran over one of her cats yesterday," Amy explained to Jimmy. "Tried to cut off its tail!"

"That true, Ronnie? You really ran over one of her cats?" Jimmy's mouth was pulled into a half smile, and his eyebrows disappeared under his hair.

"It was an accident," I sputtered.

"Awesome! Did it holler?"

"It positively screamed." Amy added, "You should have heard it."

"Well, I'm impressed," Jimmy said. "Ronnie's not afraid of Mrs. Peet. She's not afraid of any old statues either. She's the bravest girl I know." He grinned at me, showing those even white teeth of his, and winked. It was a compliment too good to pass up.

Leaving my worm bucket and fish under the big lilac that grew in the ditch by the side of the road, I ran across Mrs. Peet's overgrown yard to the cement step by the front door. I half-expected to hear piano scales, but all was quiet and the house looked like nobody was home. Of course, it always looked that way. I climbed up on the porch railing and, standing on tiptoe, reached up the roof far enough to touch the cat's tail. It was hard, painted cement.

My wet sneaker made a loud squeak when it slipped off the iron railing. I fell into the shrubs below, and was suddenly attacked by the real thing.

# 3

# Tomcat's Revenge

*The brown cat hissed and hunched his back,* puffing himself out to double his size. His sharp claws raked my bare leg. Yelling, I jumped over the shrubs and bolted down the road after Amy and Jimmy, who were laughing too hard to run fast. They stopped by Smitty's mailbox and leaned on it. We all looked back at Mrs. Peet's house, but the old woman didn't come out.

"Who do you think won the fight, Ronnie? You or that old tomcat?" Jimmy asked.

"Did you notice," Amy added, "if it had a tail?" They laughed louder, and Jimmy banged his fist against the mailbox, making a hollow, ringing sound.

"Of course it had a tail!" I said. I wasn't going to tell them it looked like the same brown tabby cat that I had run over. "And you guys can knock it off."

"What are you kids doing to my mailbox?" Smitty stood near us in that camouflage hat he always wore and a pair of safety glasses. He was a retired veteran who did carpentry work in his garage. Amy and Jimmy had been laughing so loud we didn't hear him come out.

"Nothing, Mr. Smith," Jimmy said. "We were just leaving."

Turning away, we walked back to Mrs. Peet's to get my stuff. The worm bucket was right where I'd left it, but my stringer was nowhere in sight. I circled the lilac and searched in the long grass.

"Lose something?" Amy said, coming up behind me.

"My bass—it's disappeared! Someone took it while I was on Mrs. Peet's porch, and I know who that someone is." I gave Amy the dirtiest look I could manage.

"Don't stare at me like that. I didn't take your old fish," she protested.

"She couldn't have," Jimmy said. "We never left the road while you were up there, and we ran away before you did."

"Maybe it got up and walked away," Amy suggested. "Or hey, do you think Boogie could have taken it? I haven't seen him all day."

"Naw, it wasn't Boogers," Jimmy said. "My mom took him to the vet this morning. He threw up a lot yesterday. Must have been that dead carp."

"I'll bet that cat took it." Amy looked at me with a teasing glint in her eye.

"Oh, sure," I said sarcastically.

"Maybe it was old lady Peet herself. I wouldn't put anything past her."

"Maybe," I admitted. Still, I was convinced it was Amy. She'd never done anything like that before, but she had changed a lot. And she had been pretty upset about getting smacked with my fish back at the cove. "I'm going home," I sniffed, and trotted away with my stuff. I was so mad at Amy, I could have punched her. I was sure I'd never catch another bass like the one I lost.

"I'm sorry about your fish," Amy said to my back. "Why don't you come to my house with us, and we can eat our sandwiches on my front porch."

"You're welcome to my sandwich, Amy," I yelled over my shoulder. "I'm not hungry."

"Hey, Ronnie." Jimmy ran in front of me and trotted backwards while he talked. "We're still going spying tonight, aren't we?" He nodded his head yes with a questioning look, his blue eyes squinting in the sun.

"Well, I guess." I could feel myself weakening. I never passed up a chance to go spying.

"You'll catch another winner," he assured me, and stepped out of my way. We both knew I wouldn't.

Smitty was still standing by his mailbox when I went past. "You'd better put some ointment on that leg of yours," he said. It was then that I noticed the scratches on my shin—long streaks of drying blood that reached almost to my ankle. I hurried home.

Dad was in the kitchen, listening to the scanner and having a late lunch.

"What happened to you?" he asked, staring at my leg.

"I fell into some bushes where I was fishing." At least the part about the bushes was the truth. He wouldn't have liked it if he knew I'd been messing around the catlady's house. Ever since I was little he'd told me to keep away from her because she wasn't friendly and probably didn't like kids.

"You must have fallen in the lake, too," he said, looking at my muddy shoes.

I washed the bloody scratches at the kitchen sink and Dad rubbed some first aid cream into them, making them burn like fire. "I've been doing this kind of thing all day," he said, "but I didn't expect to be doing it at home."

"Trouble on the lake?" I asked.

"There were six fishermen and an Irish setter in a twelve-foot boat that was designed to hold four. The dog fell out and everybody on board leaned over to one side to grab him. The craft tipped over, of course, and threw the whole bunch in the water. Luckily they were in the shallows by the state park, and everybody just waded to shore, except for the dog. He howled and thrashed around the overturned boat, determined to climb back up on it. I had to rescue him, and he wasn't very cooperative. The only reason I came home for lunch was so I could change into a dry uniform."

The thought of my dad wrestling a frantic Irish setter to shore was enough to make me feel better. Missing out on the fish contest didn't seem quite as awful, but I was still mad at Amy.

# 4

# Spying

*After supper that night, I* sat on the dock behind my house, throwing corn to a mother merganser and her babies. The kernels sank when they hit the water, and the ducklings dove after them, head down, sometimes disappearing completely. The lake was so peaceful that our old, wooden Chris Craft and the sleek, fiberglass patrol boat barely rubbed against their dock bumpers. Most of the holiday boaters had left the water, either to dress for dinner at Mallard's Landing or to barbecue over campfires at the state park.

The screen door banged, and I looked across the strip of neatly mowed crabgrass that was my backyard, to the porch. Amy was there. She walked out to the dock and stood, looking down at me.

"It's getting dark," she said, pulling a comb out of her hip pocket and running it through her bangs. The rest of her hair was swept off her face and rolled into twin braids that circled her head and joined in the back. It must have taken her hours to fix, I thought, not to mention her makeup, complete with eye shadow. We were both dressed in black, for spying, but Amy's designer jeans made her legs look long, and her stomach, smooth and flat. Next to her, I felt like a scrawny stick, and my old sweat suit looked like rags. "Jim should be here soon," she went on. I ignored her and tossed more corn. Across Sandglass, lights were beginning to twinkle along the shoreline.

"Okay, out with it. What's wrong?" she asked.

"You're supposed to be my best friend."

"I am," she said.

"Well, you haven't been acting like it." I threw the last handful of corn to the ducks.

"What are you talking about?"

"Did you take my bass?" I looked up at her.

"Of course not," she snapped. "How can you even think such a thing?"

"Do you swear?"

"Do you swear you didn't smack me with it on purpose to embarrass me in front of Jim?"

"Absolutely not," I said. "It was an accident, I

31

swear it." I put my left hand over my heart and held up the right. The ducklings were circling the end of the dock, quacking softly, while the mother floated nearby. I waved my empty hands at them.

Amy sat down beside me, carefully dangling her feet over the water, so her shoes wouldn't get wet. "Okay, Ronnie, I swear, too." She put one hand over her heart and held the other one up with a serious look on her face. "But it hurts my feelings that you think I would steal your fish, when I'm really sorry it's gone."

Are you? I wondered. She had to be telling the truth about the fish, though, because she never swore unless she meant it.

"Truce?" I said, spitting on two fingers and holding them out to her.

Amy looked at them, curled her lips, then spit on her fingers and rubbed them on mine. "Truce." Then she leaned down and washed her hand off in the water. With the sudden movement, the mother duck quacked loudly and led her babies away.

"Look at this," I said, rolling up my pant leg to show the red scratches.

"Wow! Those are evil-looking. You won't look good in short-shorts for a week."

"I never wear short-shorts, Amy. Is that all you can think about anymore? You've changed so much since last summer; it's like you're a different person."

"I've outgrown a lot of this kid stuff, that's all. But

32

don't worry." She put her hand on my shoulder. "My mom says we all grow up at different rates, and you'll catch up real soon."

"I'm not worried," I said, twisting my shoulder away from her hand. I had no intention of catching up soon. "But what about our being best friends? What about Clamdiggers forever?"

"You're still my absolutely best friend ever." Amy put her arm around me and gave me a hug. "The three of us will always be the Clamdiggers, but you've got to understand that Jim is . . . well, sort of my boyfriend now. I can't help it if I like him and he likes me."

"What makes you think he's *your* boyfriend?" I asked.

"Today, after you went home from Mrs. Peet's, I was carrying the cooler back to my house," she explained. "Jimmy put his hand right over mine on the handle and kept it there all the way home. And don't forget—he tried to feel around yesterday at the pier."

"He was feeling around with me, too," I said.

"Come off it, Ronnie. You're just saying that because you're jealous."

"I'm just saying that because it's true, Amy Parrish, and besides, who'd want Jimmy for a boyfriend anyway? He's more like an older brother."

"Whooo whooo whooo," a soft voice called from the side of my house. Amy and I jumped up and ran toward the sound. When we reached the corner of the garage, Jimmy stepped out. He was wearing dark jeans and a black sweatshirt. A black scarf tied tightly around his head hid his blond hair so he would blend in with the night. I thought he looked like a pirate.

"All you need is a gold earring," I teased.

"Ready to go?" he asked, staring at Amy's tight sweater. She noticed and stood up straighter.

"Where should we go first?" Amy said.

"How about Kowalskis'?" Jimmy suggested. "They went to a movie and my sister is there sitting the twins. I'll bet she has her boyfriend over." For the summer Margo was the Kowalskis' full-time babysitter. She took care of Jessie and Jeff while their parents worked, and babysat some nights, too.

"Naw, that's no fun," I said. "Margo will just complain to your mother, and besides, I don't want to scare the twins."

"We could go back to my house," Jimmy offered. "Dad's having a meeting of the Harbor Island Home-owner's Association."

"That's so boring," Amy replied. "And my folks are there."

"Then let's go next door to Smitty's," I suggested. "We could climb up the TV antenna and stomp across his roof. That always gives him a thrill."

"Naw." Amy vetoed that idea, too. "The last time we did that he gave *us* a thrill, chasing us all around the island with that baseball bat."

"That wasn't a bat; it was a tennis racquet," Jimmy corrected her. "He just wanted to scare us out of doing it again."

"Face it, you guys," Amy said. "We've been spying on the people on this island for years now and it just isn't fun anymore . . . that is, unless . . ."

"Unless what?" Jimmy asked.

"Unless we spy on the one person we almost never spy on—old lady Peet."

"Wait a minute, Amy." I reminded her, "We don't spy on the catlady because first of all, we're all supposed to stay away from there, and second of all, the couple of times we've tried it, she spotted us watching her."

"That will make it a real challenge," Jimmy said. "Let's go!" He took off with Amy down the beach before I could say one word. I caught up with them at the wire fence that separated Smitty's property from ours. Smitty had put up the fence so that it ran out into the water, forcing you to choose between getting wet or climbing over.

Amy's choice was climbing over. Jimmy put his hands together to make a step for her. Amy's jeans were so tight that I thought they'd split, but she stepped into his hands and gracefully hopped to the other side. Jimmy vaulted over after her and repeated his gallant act when we got to the other side of Smitty's lawn. This put us in the shadow of the big willow that grew just inside Mrs. Peet's yard. We could see lights on in her kitchen and living room. Someone was moving around in the house.

"What do you suppose she's doing?" I wondered out loud.

"Cooking cats," Jimmy said solemnly.

"Give me a break," I hissed. When we were little, we pretended the catlady was a witch who called wild cats out of the woods, cooked them, and ate them for supper.

"I dare you to go up and peek, Ronnie," Amy challenged. Actually I was dying to spy on the catlady, but getting scratched by her cat had dampened my enthusiasm.

"You go, Amy," I said. "Or are you chicken?" I put my hands under my arms and flapped them like wings.

"Okay, I will. You can stay here where it's safe. Jim and I will go together. Come on," Amy whispered to Jimmy. They ran, hunched over, to the shrubbery just below the kitchen window. I watched as they squatted there, frozen in place for a minute. Then they stood up, peered into the window, and came running back to me.

"What was she doing?" I asked.

"You'll never believe it in a million years," Amy said.

"What, what?"

"She was stirring something on the stove," Jimmy answered.

36

"Yes, and sitting right in the middle of the kitchen table was a cat with a cast on its tail," Amy added.

It couldn't be, I thought. It just couldn't. Whoever heard of putting a cast on a cat's tail? "Come on, you guys," I said. "That's not true and you know it."

"It's true, Ronnie. Tell her, Jimmy." Amy poked him playfully in the ribs.

"Well, it looked like a cast to me," he said, grinning.

"Do you swear, Amy?"

"Cross my heart." With her fingers, she traced a big X over her chest.

"Yeah, but do you swear?"

"Sometimes," she said, rolling her eyes at Jimmy.

"Shhh, look." Jimmy pointed to a gray and white cat that was walking in the moonlight along the beach. It cut through the yard very close to us and crept onto the back step where it sat by the door.

"Let's get out of here before old lady Peet comes out," he said. Jimmy lead the way through the catlady's back yard to the Crowleys' next door, where we stopped to sit on their glider. Catching our breath, we heard voices and sounds of an outboard motor carry in from the lake. Red and blue lights moved over the water and finally disappeared up the coast.

"Who do we want to spy on next?" I asked.

"Nobody," Amy replied. "My mom said to be in by nine."

"Since when?" In previous summers we were always allowed out until ten.

"You remember, you were there when she said it." Amy winked.

"I can take a hint," I said.

Scowling at me, Amy stood up. "Walk me the rest of the way home, Jim?"

"Uh, okay," he agreed.

"Good night, Ronnie," Amy purred, heading down the beach toward her house.

"Yeah, see ya," Jimmy said, shrugging his shoulders and hurrying after her.

When they were gone, I rocked back and forth in the glider, listening to the soft lap-lapping of the lake. I swore I'd never get as sappy over a boy as Amy did over Jimmy. And what were they doing at her house, anyway? I wondered. It was time to do some spying on my own.

# 5

# Fish Stew

*Crouching low behind the Martins' hedge at* the edge of Amy's yard, I could see those two clams in the moonlight, sitting on the dock, looking out over the lake. Once in a while, Amy would throw her head back and laugh softly. I had to know if they were talking about me.

Crawling on my stomach across the grass to the storage shed, I peeked around the side. Now only a few yards from them, I could see things clearly. Jimmy took the scarf off his head and laid it on the dock. Amy picked it up and tied and untied it, over and over. Then Jimmy said something about a song he liked, and Amy started humming softly. Finally, Jimmy slipped his arm around her, and she put her cheek against his. They talked in little whispers that were lost in the sound of the water washing against the dock pilings. I wondered if Jimmy would try to kiss her.

At least ten minutes went by and Amy and Jimmy never moved—just sat there with their cheeks glued together like Siamese twins. It was so boring that I crept back to the hedge, slipped past it, and headed for home. Walking along the Crowleys' beach, I heard something moving on the sand behind me. I turned and saw a low silhouette trotting toward me. Too big for a cat, it was Boogie, and it looked like he had something in his mouth.

"Boogie, what have you got there?" He came to me and gently laid a dead muskrat at my feet. Sitting, he wagged his tail and offered me a paw to shake.

"Ugh, Boogers, you stinky old dog. I don't want your prize," I said, backing away from him. Seeing that I wasn't going to pet him, he picked the muskrat up and trotted away.

When I reached Mrs. Peet's, the living room and kitchen lights were still on, and I thought about the cat with the cast on its tail. Amy had to be lying about the cast, but I was still a bit worried about the cat I had run over. Who would know if I checked it out now? Creeping across Mrs. Peet's yard, I crawled into the bushes next to the back door. The gray and white cat was still sitting there.

*Creeaaakk!* The screen door opened and old lady Peet stepped outside. I held my breath and crouched lower in the shrubs.

"Oh, it's you, Aunt Hester. Do come in." The cat rubbed against the woman's thin legs and went inside. Mrs. Peet took a step forward and peered straight down into the evergreen at me. Her white hair fanned out into a halo of electrified frizz around her wrinkly face, and the porch light made her look positively inhuman. "And here's the young lady that rides down innocent kitties." She pointed a crooked finger and wagged it at me. "Do come in, too, Miss Hit-and-run."

Caught! I wanted to bolt, but instead I just squatted in the bushes like an idiot, pretending I wasn't there.

"Well, I'm not going to bite you," Mrs. Peet said, putting one hand on her hip. "You've been punished enough already for what you've done. Tomcat's claws are pretty sharp."

So the old witch knew everything, I thought. She must have had a good laugh when I fell off her front porch.

Old lady Peet leaned over her back porch railing, parted the branches of the shrubbery directly above my head, and stared down at me.

"Stand up now, young lady. You can't sit out here in the bushes all night."

The juniper scratched my face as I straightened up, feeling very embarrassed at having been caught in the act of spying. "I'm sorry about running over your cat with my bike the other day," I stammered. "It was an accident, honest."

"Well, come inside and tell that to Tomcat," replied Mrs. Peet.

"I'd better not," I said, untangling my legs from the shrub. "It's late and I've got to get home."

"That may be," the old woman said, her voice stern. "But it would be very impolite not to apologize to Tomcat, now wouldn't it?" She opened the screen door and motioned me inside.

My stomach did a flip-flop, and I stood rooted to the spot, unable to make up my mind. Should I go in or take off running? Then I remembered how Jimmy said I was the bravest girl he knew. And how Amy had tricked him into walking her home, leaving me standing alone on the beach. Amy would never be daring enough to go into the old catlady's house, I reasoned. Here was my chance to impress Jimmy, and I was going to take it. I stepped up on the porch and walked past Mrs. Peet into the kitchen.

"Sit down, young lady," she said, pointing to a chair at the rectangular kitchen table. I sat, looking up at her. It was the first time I had ever seen her face up close. Her eyes were a watery blue-gray, and the loose skin on her cheeks and forehead had brown spots here and there.

"You're the Windslow girl, aren't you?" she said,

turning away to stir something on the stove. I nodded. "Tell me your first name."

"Ronnie."

"Ronnie? That's a boy's name. You look like a girl to me."

"I am a girl, and Ronnie is short for Veronica."

"Well, why didn't you say so? I will call you Veronica. Ronnie is not a proper name for a young lady, not even for a sneaky one that spies on people and runs down innocent cats." Mrs. Peet's back was to me and her voice was sharp, but I had the feeling she was smiling. "You can call me Fern. And since you're here, you can join me and my family for supper." Turning toward me, she rolled up the sleeve of the baggy cardigan that covered her faded house dress. It was the same dress she'd had on earlier in the day.

Supper? At nine-thirty at night? Looking around I realized I had taken the only empty chair in the place. The others were full of cats, sitting quietly, waiting. Something bumped against my leg, and one cat jumped into my lap. When I recognized the big brown tabby that had attacked me that afternoon, I froze, my fingers tight around the arms of the chair.

"That's Tomcat," Mrs. Peet explained. "The one you need to apologize to."

Tomcat sat quietly twitching the end of his tail. It looked all right to me. "Sorry about your tail, Tomcat." I felt silly, apologizing to a cat. His front paws danced up and down on my leg, and his claws went in and out. I gripped the arms of that chair so tightly my fingers turned white, and I could feel the puffy scratches on my leg throbbing under my sweat pants.

"Tomcat forgives you," Mrs. Peet said. "You're in his chair, but don't worry, he doesn't mind sharing." She got some plates from a dirty stack in the sink and set them around the table. Taking a large saucepan from the stove, she held it over each plate while spooning out a thick, gloppy stew. I noticed that her knobby hands were clawlike, the knuckles swollen and distorted. Slowly, awkwardly, she dished out the stew. It was mostly a gray sauce, with big white lumps, and smaller green lumps that looked like peas.

The cats hopped on the table and began to eat, each from a separate plate. Tomcat stood with his front paws on the table and his hind feet on my leg, while he licked at his dinner. He wasn't paying any attention to me, so I loosened my death grip on the chair. Still, I was careful not to move in case I disturbed him.

"Let me introduce you to the rest of my family," Mrs. Peet said. She pointed with the spoon as she named each member of the pack. "The three black and brown cats are the Woods Brothers. They are wild and come only at supper time. Fatcat," she continued, pointing to a black and white one with a huge stomach. I couldn't help but smile a little as I recognized the famous road-sleeper. "Aunt Hester, Birdy, Uncle Newt, Cousin Jake, Brother Blackie, and . . . oh dear. Where's Toothless?" She put the spoon down and looked under the table. "There you are." Bending over, Mrs. Peet picked up a smoke gray cat and put him on the table next to her plate. "He's almost as old as I am in cat years," she said as she sat and began to eat. "I have to mash his food for him." Picking a white chunk out of her stew, she squished it with a fork and laid it on the table. Toothless quickly devoured it.

"Have some stew," she offered, her mouth full, gravy dribbling down her chin. "Tomcat won't mind. Besides, it's special tonight. Birdy finally made herself useful and brought us a lovely fresh fish. Of course she was going to be a pig about it and eat it all by herself, but I convinced her to share it with the rest of us."

I watched Tomcat, happily eating the sticky mess in front of me. Did she really expect me to share a plate with him? "No thank you, Mrs. Peet, I've already eaten."

"Fern—you're supposed to call me Fern—and you don't know what you're missing. Fresh fish is very dear, and this was such a big one. It must have weighed as much as Birdy herself. It's a wonder how she managed, but Birdy is quite a determined kitty."

Fresh fish! What was that she said . . . the cat

brought home a fish? I watched Tomcat pick out a lump and chew it. Mrs. Peet's words finally sunk in—my largemouth bass was cat food!

"I'm sorry that I don't have any dessert this evening. We don't have chocolate cake or anything like that."

"Oh . . . er . . . that's all right, Mrs. Peet," I mumbled.

"Fern, remember?"

"Okay, Fern." I wasn't used to calling grown-ups by their first names, but it seemed to make her happy. Looking around the kitchen, I saw an old refrigerator, gas stove, and kitchen sink side by side in a row. Wooden cupboards hung above a counter that was cluttered with old plastic bread bags, newspapers, dirty utensils, bits of aluminum foil, unwashed dishes, and a large ball made of pieces of string. The last piece, wound tightly around the outside of the ball had a shiny metal end—my stringer!

I was too surprised to ask for it back. Instead I simply said, "I'd better go home now. My mom will be wondering where I am." Tomcat had finished cleaning his plate, and was now sitting in my lap, licking his whiskers.

When I didn't move, Mrs. Peet said, "Oh, it's okay to pick him up. Tomcat knows you're sorry about his tail. I can tell."

I took a chance. Gently stroking the fur on his back, I slipped my hand under his tummy. He hunched and

46

began to purr, so I kept on. Carefully, I lifted his head and front paws toward the table. All of a sudden, he leaped out of my hands and perched next to his plate. I stood up quickly.

Mrs. Peet got up, too, to see me to the door, and I noticed for the first time how small and frail she was. She was so short that I could look down at the top of her head, where two flat hairpins kept the frizz pulled back from her face.

"Good night, Veronica. Come back and see us sometime." She waved.

I looked down at her feet. She was wearing old holey tennies with no socks, and parts of her toes showed through the shoes. "Goodnight Mrs. . . . er . . . Fern," I said, hurrying into the dark.

"Holy guacamole!" I exclaimed to myself as I walked down the beach toward home. My mother was right about the catlady being eccentric. Still, she didn't seem dangerous or anything. And my fish! Wouldn't Jimmy be surprised about that.

"What were you doing in there, Ronnie?" said a familiar voice. I nearly jumped out of my skin, then saw it was only Jimmy at my side.

"You shouldn't sneak up on people like that," I complained.

"I didn't sneak. You weren't paying attention. Now, what *were* you doing in there?"

47

"Talking to Fern."

"Fern? Old lady Peet's name is Fern?"

"That's right, and she invited me to visit her again."

"Incredible! But why did you go in there?" Since I had Jimmy's complete attention, I walked faster. "Come on. Tell me, Ronnie," he begged, jogging sideways next to me. After we climbed over the fence, I stopped under a tree in Smitty's yard.

"I just wanted to see if you and Amy were telling the truth about the cat's tail, and you weren't," I replied, backing up against the tree and facing him.

"Aw, we were teasing and you knew it," Jimmy defended himself. "Now, tell me about old lady Peet. Is she really crazy?"

I knew I could hook him. "She does some pretty weird stuff, but I think she's mostly lonesome," I answered, trying to sound casual. "She serves her cats food at the table and shares her own plate with a really old one that doesn't have any teeth."

"Far out!" Just as casual, Jimmy put his hand on the trunk right above my shoulder and leaned toward me. He stared hard, into my eyes.

"I think she's poor, too," I rattled on. "One of her cats—Birdy is its name—stole my fish, and Fern made it into cat food."

"You're kidding?" Jimmy said. His interest in my story seemed to be waning. He put his other hand against the tree, trapping me between his arms.

48

"No, I'm not, and I had to sit there and watch them eat it. Funny thing is, though, I was mad when I thought Amy took it, but Fern, well, I just feel sorry for her, living there alone with those cats. She calls them her family."

"You going back again?" Jimmy asked, his eyes looking directly into mine. I noticed that, in the moonlight, they looked bluer than usual. It made me nervous, standing there between his arms, his breath on my face.

"I don't know. My folks would absolutely kill me if they knew I went in Fern's house, but I'm glad I did."

Jimmy moved toward me so slowly, I was surprised to see that we were almost nose-to-nose.

"You're a very daring girl, Ronnie," he whispered. When he spoke, his lips brushed mine ever so lightly. They were warm and dry, not as repulsive as I thought they would be. Was it a kiss or an accident? I decided it was a kiss. I mean, our mouths actually touched. And he'd said I was daring. Did he like daring as much as gorgeous?

"I've got to go in now," I said, and ducked under his arm. Leaving him alone, I ran across Smitty's beach and around the fence into my yard, not caring that along the way I soaked my sweat pants up to the knees with lake water.

# 6

# Sinking's Too Good for Them

*Tuesday morning all the holiday boaters* were gone, and Amy, Jimmy, and I were free to go out on the lake. Bright and early, I met Amy at her house. We were going to pick up Jimmy in her dad's new boat.

Amy and I watched from the dock while Mr. Parrish took the canvas cover off the *Amy Mae*. When he had finished, he stepped back and said, "Now that's what I call a first-class fishing boat!"

I suppose he was right about that, but the sleek, twenty-foot craft was also one terrific ski boat. Amy and I hopped aboard. It was perfect weather for skiing: sunny and almost no wind.

"Just remember, Amy," her dad said. "Even though I had her out fishing over the weekend, she's still not completely broken in. Keep her real slow all the way to Jimmy's so she'll be running smooth by the time you get to the ski lane."

"Sure thing, Dad," Amy answered, settling into the captain's chair. I sat in the bucket seat on the passenger side, and Mr. Parrish gave the bow a push with his foot, tossing the rope to me. Then Amy started the powerful inboard-outboard engine and backed away from the dock. As she drove up the coast at five miles per hour, she said, "Do you think Jim will like my hair this way?" Her curls had been slicked back flat and pulled into a neat little topknot that made her cheekbones stick out. "It's the wet look, just like they wear for synchronized swimming on TV."

"He'll just drool." I sighed.

As we passed the Crowleys, we saw the Kowalski twins hanging over the end of the dock. Jessie was tossing something in the water, and Jeff was wildly waving a big net around. Kneeling behind them and holding their ankles was Margo.

"They're feeding doughballs to the carp and trying to catch one," I said. "Remember when we used to do that?"

"Yeah, but I'd rather do other stuff now."

"Like what?"

"Like go to the movies or out on dates."

51

"You've never been on a date, Amy."

"Well, Jim and I are kind of dating," she said. "Remember the other night when you had to go in early and he walked me home?"

I swiveled my seat around to face her. "I didn't have to go in early, and that was no date, Amy."

"Well, it was sort of like a date. We sat out on the dock, Jim put his arm around me, and we stared into each other's eyes in the moonlight." She looked straight ahead and kept both hands on the wheel. "You wouldn't believe how romantic Jim's eyes look in the moonlight!"

I knew exactly how his eyes looked in the moonlight. "Did he kiss you?" I asked.

"That's personal."

"Well, he kissed *me*," I said, leaning toward her for emphasis.

Amy put her hand on the throttle and increased our speed to ten miles per hour. We passed Fern's house, then Smitty's, then mine. I noticed that our grass needed cutting.

"He couldn't have kissed you," Amy said. "You weren't even alone with him."

"After you two went on your 'date,' I went to Fern's house."

"Who's Fern?" she asked, glancing at me.

"Mrs. Peet. She wants me to call her Fern."

"You mean she talked to you?"

"Yeah. I went in her house and everything. She introduced me to all her cats, and . . . you lied to me, Amy. That cat didn't have a cast on its tail."

"You mean you really went in her house?" Amy tapped her fingers against the steering wheel.

So then I told her all about Fern's "family" and the fish stew. While I was talking, we passed a long string of cottages and rounded the southern end of the island.

As soon as I was through, Amy said, "You see, I didn't lie about taking your fish. And I think you'd better not hang around that nutty woman anymore. Your mom would have a fit if she knew."

"Fern didn't do anything wrong, and I kind of like her." Besides, I thought, talking to Fern was more fun than sitting in Amy's new boat, listening to her go on about her "date."

"Like her? A crazy old woman who lives in a filthy house and roams all around the woods with her cats? And she stole your fish—the one you accused me of stealing."

"She didn't steal it. It was the cat. . . ."

Now we were in sight of the Jackmans' dock and could see Jimmy waving at us with one hand, his skis in the other. As Amy cut the engine, she leaned over to me and whispered, "You lied about the kiss."

*    *    *

On the way to the ski lane, Jimmy kept talking about how great the new boat was, and how he couldn't wait to drive her, but I got behind the wheel instead. That was because Amy wanted to ski first, and she insisted that Jimmy be her spotter. Tossing her skis in the water, Amy gave me a stern warning to drive her namesake carefully. Then she jumped in. I eased the boat forward slowly to tighten the tow rope.

"Hit it," Jimmy said. He was standing behind my seat facing backwards, watching Amy. I shoved the throttle all the way forward, and the boat shot ahead. "She's up," Jimmy reported to me. Easing back to twenty-five miles per hour, I concentrated on the water ahead. "She's over the wake."

Turning my head, I saw Amy sail out to the side of the boat. She was leaning away from the rope for speed.

I enjoyed being at the wheel, and there wasn't another boat in sight. The fiberglass hull of the *Amy Mae* cut through the smooth water like a knife through jelly, and her engine purred like a contented cat. While Amy turned and shot back across our wake, I thought again of Fern, and smiled. Circling the end buoy, I steered the boat toward the other side of the ski lane.

"Check this out," Jimmy called. I turned to look, just as Amy dropped one ski and put her free foot

54

through the rope handle. She leaned back and threw her arms wide to the sides.

"Look at that. Isn't she great?" he exclaimed.

Show-off, I thought. Did he like her skiing or her bathing suit the best?

Circling the buoys again, I drove back to the spot where the dropped ski was floating, coasted close to it, and let Amy down easy. She grabbed the ski and swam to the boat.

Then it was my turn. I slid my slalom into the water and jumped in after it. I knew I could beat Amy on one ski any day. Jimmy tightened the line and hit it. I came up easy. Funny, I didn't hear Amy warn him about being careful.

Waving at them, I zigzagged back and forth, jumping the wake. But while Jimmy was watching where he was driving, Amy was watching him instead of me. She stared at Jimmy, her chin on his shoulder. I even did (perfectly) Amy's trick of holding the rope with my foot. That didn't get their attention, either.

"Hey hey heeey!" I yelled. They were about to see something they wouldn't soon forget—something none of us had dared before. I was going to ski barefoot.

Bending down slightly, I loosened my ski's binding. Then, taking a big breath, I stepped off my ski, leaned back, and braced my feet against the rushing water. To my surprise, I lasted in this position for about five seconds. Then I flew straight up in the air and flipped completely over. When I hit the water with a giant smack, it felt as hard as a rock. I sank, but my ski belt brought me back up to the surface and I bobbed there, trying to breathe normally. My head felt like someone had clubbed me with a baseball bat, and my whole right side was numb. But for five seconds I had given a glorious performance! Alas, there had been no audience.

I watched the *Amy Mae* speed away from me. My spotter's arm was around Jimmy, her chin still resting on his shoulder. Both were completely unaware that they had lost me. I screamed for them to stop, but I guess they didn't hear. Nor did they seem to have noticed the water-logged tree trunk that had floated into the ski lane. I heard a dull thunk when the boat drove over it, and the engine's shrill scream just before it died. The *Amy Mae* coasted to a stop and sat, dead in the water.

The boat was maybe three hundred feet away and I could just make out what Amy and Jim were shouting to each other.

"What was *that?*" Amy said, peering into the water at the rear of the boat. Jimmy leaped over the back of the captain's chair and leaned over the stern next to her.

"It's a floater," he said, pointing to the bobbing log nearby.

"Do you think it hurt anything? What if we have a hole in the bow? What if she *sinks?*" Amy cried.

"Hey, what happened to Ronnie?" Jimmy looked panicked. *"Ronnie!"* He scanned the ski lane with his hand above his eyes. I was so mad at them now that I dog-paddled a few yards and hid behind a buoy. Serves them right, I thought. My ski floated close by, and I reached out and grabbed it.

"What are we going to *do?*" Amy yelled, crawling into the driver's seat.

"Try to start her up. We've got to go back and look for Ronnie."

The engine kicked in, but the boat didn't go anywhere. The motor just whined higher and higher until Amy shut it off. "Now *what?*" She glared at Jimmy, who was still searching the ski lane.

"The engine works, but I think we lost the prop," he explained. "We're going to have to wait for a tow."

I couldn't quite make out Amy's next words because they came out in a moan. The meaning, though, was "My dad's going to kill us both!"

I want a ringside seat when that happens, I thought.

"At least we're not sinking," Jimmy said. *"Ronnie!"* he called again. I was pleased that Jimmy seemed more worried about me than Amy's precious boat.

"I'm scared, Jim," Amy said, picking up the cue. "What on earth could have happened to Ronnie?"

It's taken you long enough to wonder, I thought. Sinking's too good for you. My head still ached, but the feeling had come back in my right side, and I could breathe better. Those two needed a lesson, and I was going to give them one they'd never forget.

My side of the ski lane was maybe a quarter mile from Murky Cove. I thought I could make it swimming. Without my white ski vest, I'd be almost impossible to see from the boat. Slipping it off, I wrapped it around my ski and buckled it to the chain that anchored the buoy. My plan was to get to shore, go home, and get the Chris Craft to rescue my "good" friends. In the meantime, I'd enjoy letting them sit there in the hot sun thinking I'd drowned.

After swimming for only a few minutes, I could see that my revenge wasn't going to come easy. A stiff wind blew up, turning the water choppy, and the current carried me in the wrong direction, up the coast. My right shoulder became so sore that I had to change from the crawl to the side stroke.

"Ronnie, Ronnie!" Jimmy's voice grew fainter. By the time my feet finally touched bottom, it was oozy mud, and I had to fight my way through thick mats of water lilies. The current had pulled me completely off course into a tiny, secluded cove. I couldn't see the boat anymore, and Jimmy's voice had faded out completely. I was alone in the big bog.

*Whoosh!* A rush of flapping wings startled me. Three birds took off nearby. They were greenish, with long legs and bills—a kind I had never seen before. Three more were wading in the lilies, folding up their long legs, one at a time, to clear the shallow water.

Picking my way through the bog, the mud sucking at my feet, I wondered if there was any quicksand around.

The muck changed to a thick peat with low-growing plants, and the musky stench of skunk cabbage filled the air. Gradually the ground got firmer, tamaracks gave way to large pines, and I realized I was in the woods beyond the bog—the one that Jimmy, Amy, and I had longed to explore. How was I going to get home now? I asked myself. I knew I couldn't be too far from the trail by Murky Cove. But to get there I would have to cross the bog. Somehow, I really had screwed things up now. Instead of rescuing Amy and Jimmy, I was the one who needed rescuing.

Completely lost, I sat down on a log in a small clearing to think things through. The rough bark cut into my bare legs. At my feet I saw several mounds of green plants growing in neat rectangles.

"Come down here, you naughty girl," a nearby voice said. Looking up, I saw Mrs. Peet, standing a few yards from me, waving her finger at a pine tree. I was relieved to see someone, anyone.

"Are you talking to me, Mrs. Peet?"

Clearly, she was as surprised to see me as I was to see her. But she recovered almost instantly.

"Fern. You're supposed to call me Fern," she replied "and I'm talking to Birdy, who's being very stubborn right now. What are *you* doing in my woods?" She motioned for me to come closer.

As I walked toward her, I noticed that her tennies were perfectly dry. She must have seen my feet, too—mud up to the ankles.

"You have to know where to step," she observed, her watery eyes shining, her thin lips pulled back tight at the corners. "Goodness, you're a sight!" I couldn't help smiling. Fern was "a sight" herself with her hair sticking straight out and that baggy sweater hanging down to her knees.

"I've been swimming." It was cold in the shade, and goose bumps were popping up all over me.

"Oh dear," Fern said. She took off the brown sweater and wrapped it around my shoulders. The wool was scratchy and had a strong smell like moth balls and rotten potatoes. I wanted to take it off, but I didn't want to hurt her feelings. And it was warm.

"Thanks," I said.

"Sit down and join our picnic." Making herself comfortable on a stump, the old woman picked up her shiny pail. "Let's see," she said. "Here's a piece of bread, and some fresh mint. Unfortunately, the straw-berries are all gone. Too bad we didn't find anything for dessert, but chocolate cake doesn't grow on trees." Suddenly, Toothless appeared from out of nowhere. He jumped on Fern's lap and licked her on the chin. "My, my, it's been years since I've had a chocolate cake." She looked thoughtful for a brief moment then gave a little cackle and held the pail out to me.

Ugh! I thought, looking at the collection of leaves and bread chunks. "No, thank you." I tried to sound gracious.

We heard a rustling from the pine as an orange tabby cat emerged, tail first, and ambled over to Fern.

"Well, I guess it's all right, Birdy. I found my lunch in the woods and so did you. However, you could at least wipe the evidence off your face." She bent over, ran a knotty finger along the cat's lips, and held up a small brown feather. "Song sparrow," she said sadly, shaking her head. "I'm glad it wasn't one of the green heron. They're my favorite." She turned her head and looked up at me. "I love birds, but unfortunately Birdy does too—in a different way."

"There were some greenish birds with long legs, wading in the lily pads. Are they the green heron?" I asked.

"Exactly. That little cove is the only place on the island where they live. I call it Hidden Cove, because until now, nobody but me knew it was there." She stood up and pointed to the mounds of green plants that now looked suspiciously like catnip. "And now here you are. Right in the middle of my sacred ground."

Sacred ground? I was going to have a fantastic story to tell Jimmy and Amy! That's when I remembered that they were still sitting out on the lake in the *Amy Mae.*

"I have to hurry home," I said. "Can you tell me where the trail to Murky Cove is?"

"Lost, are you?" She smiled. "If you really must know, it's over that way." She waved her hand vaguely. "But I'd better take you. You look like you've had enough adventures for one day. Come children, it's time to go." As Mrs. Peet picked up the pail, several cats appeared like magic.

She moved quickly through the trees to the edge of the bog, and led me over the swampy ground. Expertly, she avoided stepping in the mucky places. Soon the ground became firmer, the trees taller, and I knew we were on the Murky Cove trail.

"I can get home from here," I said, and Fern stopped. "I've never been to the woods beyond the bog before. Thanks for showing me the way out."

"You can come back any time you like, but don't tell anyone else about this place." Then Fern stepped close to me and looked up, into my eyes. "I don't want a whole parade of people back there. Especially not around my sacred ground." Then she retreated back into the woods.

# 7

# Grounded

*From Beach Road, I could see the county* sheriff's car parked right behind Mom's station wagon. Sheriff Hughes never came to the house unless there was trouble. How long had I been lost in the bog? What time was it, anyway? I wondered, looking up at the sky. What if there had been a hole in the *Amy Mae?* What if she sank?

I ran up the driveway, jumped on the step, and jerked open the door. My mother was standing in the kitchen crying into a paper towel, and Sheriff Hughes had his arms around her.

*"Veronica!"* Mom threw herself at me, grabbing me into a hug so tight I thought my ribs would crack.

"You're here! You're all right! Where on earth have you been? I thought you'd drowned and *phew*! What's that awful smell?" Her words came out in a rush. She stepped back and held me at arm's length. Her face was red and puffy. I realized that I was still wearing Fern's sweater and that I was in a lot of trouble.

"Answer me right now," Mom said. Her eyes, no longer teary, had that glint that signaled fury.

Casually, I took the sweater off and laid it over the back of a kitchen chair. "It's just an old rag I found lying on the beach. I was cold, so I put it on." This was not the time to tell her about Fern.

"I don't care about the sweater. Where have you been?"

"Yes, Ronnie. Where have *you* been?" Sheriff Hughes asked. "We were just about ready to start dredging the ski lane. Your dad picked up Amy and Jimmy well over an hour ago, and we searched everywhere for you. They're still out there looking for you. Your ski and vest were floating off the point, way over by the old stone pier."

I didn't know where to begin. I knew whatever I said would sound lame. "I tied them to a buoy. They must have gotten away."

"You know better than to take off your life vest in deep water," Sheriff Hughes lectured. "What made you think you could swim easier without it?" He stared hard at me with a stern look on his face. "Your dad thought you slipped out of your vest and went under. He radioed me and I sent Deputy Loomis in the other patrol boat to help search for you. Mr. Hadley and a couple of men from the marina are out there, too." He stopped talking and waited for an explanation. I didn't have a good one.

"Well, I tried to ski barefoot and had a bad fall. Jimmy ran over an old log, and the boat conked out before they could come back to pick me up."

Mom's expression didn't change. "Go on, Veronica."

"I had to swim to shore." I put my head down to avoid looking at Sheriff Hughes. "I guess it was stupid to leave my vest behind like that. On the way home to get our boat, I got lost in the woods beyond the bog. I never would have got out of there without . . . er . . . without luck."

"Just look at you," my mother said, shaking her head. "Your whole leg is black-and-blue, your feet are all scraped up and covered with mud, and there's a big lump on your forehead."

I felt my head with my fingers. Sure enough, there was a lump just above one eye. When I touched it, my headache came back. "The rope handle must have hit me when I fell."

"I'm going up to the pier to find your two friends and take them home," Sheriff Hughes said. "They're with the deputies combing the shore for you, and they're awful upset. I'll radio your dad from the car." Turning to Mom, he changed his tone. "I'm glad everything worked out all right."

All right? I wondered if anything would ever be all right again. My folks were going to be boiling mad for a long time. And Jimmy and Amy would probably never speak to me again.

That night, my parents had one of their "little talks" with me. My dad sat at the end of the kitchen table, drumming his fingers while my mother sat opposite me and grilled me like I was on a witness stand. A hardened criminal wouldn't have a chance with her.

"Tell me why you swam off like that and didn't let Amy and Jimmy know you were going for help." She leaned across the table and put her finger under my chin. Lifting my head, she stared directly into my eyes. This move always worked. So I confessed everything. Except, of course, where the sweater came from, and that was only because Mom had forgotten about it. I'd hidden it in my room as soon as Sheriff Hughes left.

"I'm disappointed in your irresponsible behavior, Ronnie," Dad said, shaking his head. His fingers ceased drumming. "You can't imagine how scared I was. I've patrolled Sandglass many times for missing persons, but you've no idea how awful it is when it's your own daughter."

"We understand that you felt angry at Amy and Jimmy for ignoring you," Mom went on. "But that is no excuse to leave them stuck out in a damaged boat thinking you were dead." She took her finger away, but I could still feel the dent in my chin from her nail point.

"I'm sorry," I stammered, picking at the reed placemat in front of me. I had woven it from cattails the summer before. Now that seemed a very long time ago. "I was lost in the bog."

"You were in the bog?" Dad asked. I nodded but kept quiet. "Well, luck was really on your side today," he said drily, his finger march beginning again. "You were lucky to get out of there."

"You've given your dad and me quite a shock," Mom said. "We feel you need time to think about your actions." She looked over at Dad, and he nodded his head. "That's why we're grounding you for a week— starting tomorrow."

A whole week! I'd never been grounded for a whole week. Slowly I turned my head toward Dad and gave him the most miserable look I could manage.

"Don't squint at me," he said. "You've been punished some already by the looks of those bruises, but you pulled quite a stunt. And it won't hurt you a bit to stay home for a while and think things over. I've already given Amy a lecture about not spotting her skier, and Jimmy one about not watching where he was driving. And I'm banning all three of you from the lake until August."

Amy phoned the next morning. When I answered she said, "I just called to tell you I'm not speaking to you for the rest of the summer! And I'm telling Jim not to, either."

"Amy, wait, don't hang up," I said. There was silence on the other end, but no click, so I knew she was listening.

"I'm sorry about skipping out on you, but I was just going home to get the boat, honest. I never meant to leave you out there that long." I pulled a chair up to the kitchen counter, sat on the counter top, and put my feet in the chair. The silence on the line continued. "Look, Amy, I know you're listening, and it will probably thrill you to know that I'm grounded until next Wednesday."

"A week?" Her voice was high and loud. "If you ask me, they let you off too easy. Can you imagine how Jimmy and I felt, thinking you had drowned? Your dad gave us quite a lecture on water safety. And after all that, we're being punished, too. I guess it doesn't matter that we can't go skiing until August, because my dad won't let me take the *Amy Mae* out until then anyway. And Mr. Jackman is making Jim go to work at the marina to earn enough money to pay my dad for the new prop. This whole mess is all your fault, Ronnie."

"Now wait just a minute, Amy." I twisted the phone cord around my finger. "If you'd been spotting me like you were supposed to, this whole thing never would have happened. You were so busy batting your eyes at Jimmy, you didn't even notice that I took a bad fall. And if Jimmy had been paying attention to his driving, he wouldn't have hit that log."

"I knew I shouldn't have called you for an apology, Ronnie Windslow!" *Click*, she hung up on me.

The following week was the longest of my entire life. I cut the grass, did the laundry, cleaned my closet, and washed the windows, the car, my bike, and the Chris Craft. And while I was working, I wondered what Amy and Jimmy were doing, and if Jimmy was mad at me, too.

On Saturday, I was pulling weeds near the front door, when my two "friends" rode by on their bikes. Amy stuck her nose in the air and pretended she didn't see me. As soon as Jimmy glanced at me, she said, "Come on, Jims, let's go to my house and I'll make lemonade."

"Jims" shrugged his shoulders and took off after her. I pulled up a huge thistle and imagined Amy with some kind of disease that would force her to stay inside all summer. She would swell up and have a rash all over her face and yes, oh yes, it would cause her hair to fall out. I could picture her sitting on her front porch in a wheelchair, scarf tied around her head to hide the bald spots, blanket tucked around her bloated body. Jimmy and I would ride by on our bikes, and she would lift her feeble arm and wave weakly.

"Poor thing," Jimmy would say, turning his head so he didn't have to look at her.

"Yes, it's such a shame," I'd say. "Why don't we go to my house for lemonade?" I stopped pulling weeds when I realized I had pulled the last one and had started on the petunias.

Monday morning, Mom said to me, "I have the day off from the clinic. Want to come to town with me to do the grocery shopping?"

"No thanks, I'll stay here and mow the grass."

"But you did that two days ago. Are you sure you wouldn't like to come along?"

"I know, I'll bake a cake for dessert tonight while you're gone."

"Will wonders never cease? You want to cook?"

"I'm so bored, I'll try anything."

"Go ahead, your dad will love it."

After she left I found two cake mixes in the cupboard, one yellow and one chocolate. Stirring the brown mix made me think about Fern and how she loved chocolate cake but hadn't had any in years. Her sweater was still hidden in my room. I decided she was probably always wearing it because it was the only one she had.

I baked two cakes and frosted them with chocolate icing. I put the chocolate one in the Tupperware Cake Taker and got the sweater from my room. You shouldn't be leaving the house, screamed my conscience. I'll only be gone for a minute, I whispered guiltily.

# 8

# Fern's Surprise Visitor

*When I walked up Fern's driveway, there was* a blue Oldsmobile parked behind Mrs. Peet's beat-up old Ford. That was unusual—she never seemed to have any visitors. Even though I knew I had to get home in a hurry, I couldn't resist a little spying.

Carrying the cake, I went around the side of the one-car garage to the back of the house. Voices drifted out the open living room window. Keeping low, between the house and shrubs, I worked my way under the window.

Fern's cracked voice said, "Why don't you stay away? You never come to see me, and when you do, it's always trouble."

"You know it's a two-and-a-half-hour drive from Lansing, and besides, every time I try to help you, all you do is argue with me. Now tell me . . . what did you do with it?"

"I sold it. A few months ago," Fern replied.

Sold what? I wondered, inching closer to the window.

"Sold it?" the man asked. "I can't believe you would ever sell it. That piano was your favorite thing. How could you stand to part with it?"

A piano? I was disappointed. I was hoping for something glamorous, like a diamond necklace or a stolen painting.

"I needed the money," Fern explained in a low voice.

"Money? What happened to all the money Dad left you?"

"Oh, I spent it a long time ago."

"Spent it? Dad left you enough so you could live on the interest. And if you ran out, you should have come to me. For heaven's sake, Mother. What did you spend it on?"

Mother! It never crossed my curious mind that Fern might have children.

"Fresh fish is very dear these days," she said. "And I do have such a large family to feed."

"Family? What family?"

"Well, there's Toothless, Tomcat, Aunt Hester—"

"You mean the cats?" he interrupted.

"They're all I've got."

"No, they're not. You have me, Mother. I'm your family and I can't stand to see you living in this run-down place with cats in every corner. You don't keep yourself clean, and you eat off filthy dishes. It's a wonder you don't get food poisoning. Now you say you've spent all your money? You must be confused. There's probably some mix-up at the bank about sending you your checks."

I couldn't stand the suspense one second longer. I had to get a look at this guy, so I peeked in the corner of the window. All I saw was the back of two heads, Fern's white frizz and her son's bald spot. Baldy stood up, and showed himself to be a middle-aged man in a tweed sport jacket. He turned to face her, and I was afraid he'd see me, but he was intent on staring at Fern. The man had a red, round face and was fat. Not grossly fat, but definitely tubby. He talked in a soft, patient voice.

"Mother, I think it's time for you to come and live near Tina and me. I'll look around and see what kind of places are available."

"*What!*" she shouted. "You want to lock me up in some old folks home to die?" Standing, Fern came to only the middle of her son's chest.

"Not an old folks home—a retirement residence,"

he said. "Some of them are really nice, with maid service and meals and everything."

"I don't think the rest of the family would like that."

"I'm sorry, Mother. You can't keep animals in retirement homes." He took a step forward, bent down, and gently put his hands over hers. "I only want to help you, Mother. Why won't you let me take care of you?"

Fern grabbed his tie and pulled his face down even with hers. "Because you're always talking about putting me away somewhere and I won't go, so there! Now just get yourself back to Lansing and forget all about it."

"Okay, Mother, I'm going, but I'll be back as soon as I get some answers." He kissed her forehead. Fern let go of his tie and wiped the kiss away with the back of her hand.

The man disappeared into the kitchen for a minute.

"What are you doing snooping around in there?" she asked.

"Nothing." He came back into the living room and walked across it to the front door. When he was almost there, the man tripped over Birdy, who let out a yowl and tried to scratch him on the leg. Instead she got her claws caught in his pants. He stopped and shook her loose, but not before Birdy bit him in the ankle.

"Lord almighty!" Mr. Peet let out a yowl of his own,

hastening Birdy's escape to the kitchen. He rolled up his pant leg to check out the damage. "At least it's not bleeding," he consoled himself. After giving his leg a quick rub, he smoothed back the hem of his pants and shook his head at Fern. "I'm more convinced than ever, Mother, that I need to get you away from here."

"When Beethoven comes back from the grave!" Fern yelled. Neither of them said good-bye.

I stayed hidden in the shrubs until I heard the car drive off. Just as I was going to go around to the front, the kitchen door opened.

"You might as well come in, Veronica."

I might as well, I thought. It's impossible to sneak up on her. She knows every time.

# 9

# Piano Lesson

*How long were you listening, Miss Busy-*body?" she asked as I came inside. It was hard to tell if she was mad or just teasing. Immediately, she noticed the sweater and Cake Taker.

"Oh, you've brought me a present." Her lips crinkled into a smile.

"Here's your sweater," I said, handing it to her. "And I baked a chocolate cake for you and your family." I set it on the kitchen table next to some money that was already lying there.

"For me? And my family?" Fern had started to take the cake cover off when she noticed the bills, grabbed them, and began counting them. There were some twenties and a couple of tens—must have been over a hundred dollars. Opening a cupboard, she stuck the money in an empty jelly jar. Then she picked up a knife and a stack of dirty dishes that were next to the sink, and put them on the table by the cake.

"Come, children," she called, lifting the cover. "See what a delicious treat Veronica brought us." Cats appeared from every corner and hopped on the table. She divided the cake into thirteen equal pieces, counting as she cut. One plate held three pieces, and she shoved it into the cupboard with the money. "Those are for the wild Woods Brothers," she explained. "I hope they show up tonight." Back at the table, she pushed a plate under each cat's nose, handed me one, and took one for herself. Looking around, she realized there was one extra. "Oh, where is that Fatcat? He does so love to eat, and he would be out wandering around when we're all having cake." Sighing, she stored the extra piece next to the Woods Brothers' slices. "I'll just save it for him. Come, Veronica." She beckoned, handing me a fork. "Let's take our cake into the other room."

I knew I should leave, but I was certain Mom wouldn't be home for another half hour. Besides, it would only take a couple of seconds to check out the living room. An Early American sofa with a cat-clawed slipcover stood under the window where I had spied on Fern and her son. She sat, patted the cushion next to her, and began to eat her cake. I looked at my plate, which had bits of old food stuck to it.

"I think you'd better save my piece for Fatcat, too. Really, I'm not very hungry, and I have another cake at home." I put my share down on the scratched coffee table.

"Very well, you know best." Fern wiped a bit of icing from her chin with her sleeve. "My, my, this cake is so delicious."

While she ate, I looked around the room. Against the wall opposite the kitchen was a black upright piano. Above it hung a huge painting—one of those fancy ones in a gold frame with a light under it. A young woman in a rose-colored dress sat at the longest grand piano I had ever seen. The rest of the room was empty, except for the sofa, several stacks of yellowed sheet music, and a brass floor lamp that stood by itself in the middle of a huge Oriental rug. I wondered where all the furniture had gone.

Fern's fork made a loud clink as it hit her plate and then bounced onto the floor. The last bite of cake rolled onto her lap. "Oh, dear me, I am so clumsy, so terribly clumsy." I noticed that her face was pale and her lips were quivering.

"Are you all right?" I asked, bending down to pick up the fork.

"Of course. Visits from George always give me a headache." She took a deep breath and finished the cake that had tumbled into her lap.

"Do you think he'll do it? Make you move away?"

"I don't know. That's why I sold my beautiful D. I was running short of money, and I didn't want to ask him for it. I knew if I did, he'd come snooping around here and threaten me like that." She sat up straight and Toothless hopped in her lap.

"What's a D?"

"The Steinway Model D. It's nine feet long and the grandest of all concert pianos. Of course, I didn't get anything near what it was worth. But if I'm careful, the money will be enough to last until . . ." Her voice trailed off, and she rubbed Toothless on the top of his head. "Anyway," she continued, "the man that bought it was pleased to get such a treasure and promised to restore it." She stared at the floor lamp, which now looked lonelier than ever. I tried to imagine it sitting next to the piano in the portrait. The piano would have filled the whole room. I looked at the painting again. The woman in the rose dress was small and slim and very young, not at all like Fern. She had curly brown hair instead of white frizz, and her smooth, white skin made Fern's seem even more saggy and spotted. But the expression of the eyes, the shape of the nose . . . yes, they were the same.

Fern must have read my thoughts. She picked up

Toothless and placed him on the coffee table, where he sniffed at the cake I hadn't touched. Then, standing, she rubbed her hand over the crackled paint of the upright piano. "The D may be gone, but I still have my old practice piano here. Don't let its appearance fool you. It's a Steinway, too, and I've had it seventy-nine years, ever since I was four years old."

Wow, I thought. Amy, Jimmy, and I used to make bets on how old she was. Now I knew. "You mean you could play the piano when you were only four?"

"I was a child prodigy, and then a concert artist," Fern explained.

"A prodigy?" I couldn't wait to find out how Fern came to be in the portrait.

"Yes, you know, a child with an exceptional talent. In my case, it was music. By the time I was ten, I had won competitions all over the United States and Europe. I even gave concerts and command performances to royalty." She held up her knotty hands. "Then, when I was twenty-seven, at the peak of my career, rheumatoid arthritis got me." Leaning toward me, she shook her fists in my face. "I had the power in my hands to make people feel things, things the great composers felt when they wrote their music, and things I felt when I played it." She unclenched her hands and sat down at the piano. "Now I'm just like old Toothless without his teeth."

She began playing, so softly at first I could hardly

hear the music. Gradually, the sound became louder. It made me feel relaxed and happy. When she was finished, I asked her the name of the piece.

"That was Beethoven's Sonata op. 27, no. 2, adagio sostenuta. But most people know that section as the *Moonlight* Sonata."

I didn't recognize either name of the piece, although I had heard it several times before.

"I never play anything anymore," she said wistfully. "Just some scales now and then for old times' sake. What you just heard was nothing. You should have listened to me perform in the old days."

"I wish I could play like you can now."

"Well, you could if you practiced. Here, give it a try."

Sliding onto the bench next to her, I noticed that she smelled like her sweater, only stronger. I remembered what her son had said about her not keeping herself clean. Could he have been right about her being better off in a retirement home? Then I felt guilty for even thinking such a thing.

Fern took my hands in hers and examined them. Her skin was so clammy, and her knuckles so bumpy, I felt like something from *Creature Features* had me.

"Not bad," she said, turning my fingers over. "Not bad at all."

"You mean I could play the piano?" I hadn't given

it much thought before, but now the idea seemed exciting.

"If you'll sit still."

Fern showed me how to curve my fingers into a rounded position. She put them on the piano and had me play every key up and down, repeating the names of the notes after her. Then, from beneath the pile of sheet music, she pulled out some paper with lines on it and drew several notes on the lines. Soon she had me reading and playing "Twinkle, Twinkle, Little Star."

"I can't believe it's me, making the music," I said.

"You're doing well for your first lesson." Fern patted me on the back and smiled. I watched the wrinkles around her eyes bunch up. "I'll give you a new one every week."

Startled by the offer, I stared at her.

"What's the matter, Veronica?"

"I don't know if my mother will let me take lessons," I said slowly, "and I don't have a piano to practice on." Looking down at my hands, I took them slowly off the keys.

"Of course you must consider your mother's feelings, but Veronica, you're the one who must decide what things are important in your life," Fern replied firmly. "As for the piano, you can come here and practice every morning."

*Plink, plink, plink* went the high notes as Tomcat walked over them. We both laughed, and I pulled him into my lap. He rubbed his head against my chin and purred. I wasn't one bit afraid of him now.

*Plink, plink, plink.* Fern played the same keys. "That's a lovely theme, Tomcat." She added some chords with her left hand and turned the original three notes into a real piece of music. "What shall we call this composition?"

"How about 'Tomcat Boogie'?" I suggested.

"Excellent title. Now you play it while I write it down."

I played it over and over with Tomcat in my lap and would have gone on forever if it weren't for the car horn blasting in front of Fern's house. My stomach turned inside out and jumped into my throat. I recognized that horn.

"Fatcat must be having a nap," Fern said matter-of-factly.

Looking across the living room through the front window, I saw my mom, parked in the middle of the road, tooting away at Fatcat.

"Holy guacamole! I have to get home!" I leaped over the piano bench and dumped Tomcat on the floor in my race for the back door.

"Do come to practice again tomorrow," Fern said.

"Not till Wednesday!" I yelled as the door slammed shut behind me.

84

# 10

# Run, Ronnie, Run

*Leaping off Fern's back step, I catapulted* over the shrubs at an angle and came down running. As I tore along the beach, I counted the honks.

"Five, six, seven," I gasped. It usually took at least ten. My legs flew faster and my breath came in big gulps. I didn't want to think about what would happen if I didn't beat Mom home. I cleared the first of Smitty's fences with room to spare, but peeled a slice of skin off my ankle bone on the second. When I landed in my backyard, I heard gravel crunching in front of my house. I yanked the back screen open and threw myself in the porch swing, just as the kitchen door banged and Mom's cheery voice called out, "Ronnie, I'm home."

Pulling a pillow over my ankle, I lay in the swing, trying to catch my breath. "I'm out here," I answered. Puffing, I could hear Mom putting away the groceries. Then the doorbell rang.

"Jimmy's here to see you," Mom said, stepping out on the porch. "Goodness, you look worn out. What have you been doing?"

"I was dancing to some music on the stereo and came out here to rest."

"You can go out front to talk to Jimmy for a few minutes, but remember, you're still grounded for two more days."

After a quick trip to the bathroom for a Band-Aid, I went to the front door. Jimmy was sitting on the step. Boogie lay beside him, in the flower bed. "Hi," I said, stifling an urge to ask where Amy was. Lately she'd been stuck to Jimmy like gum. Boogie poked my hand with his wet nose, and I kneeled down to scratch him behind the ears.

"How's it going?" Jimmy asked.

"Day after tomorrow, I get out of prison." I made a face. Then I saw that Jimmy's torn jeans were spotted with grease. "How's the job at Hadley's?"

"It's okay, I guess." He looked down at his brown-edged fingernails, then up at me. "You sure scared Amy and me. We were worried about you."

"I'm sorry. It was wrong of me to leave without telling you, but I was mad."

"About what?"

"Well, skiing barefoot isn't something you do every day, and you two didn't even notice that I took a bad fall."

"You're putting me on. You didn't really ski bare-foot."

"For a few seconds I did. I swear."

"Fantastic!" he exclaimed, before turning serious again. "You're right. Amy should have been watching you." He wrinkled his forehead, and his face had a somber look. Putting his finger on my shoulder, he ran it slowly down to my elbow. "Don't ever pull another stunt like that one, Ronnie. I really thought you had drowned or something."

My whole arm tingled where he touched it. "I was going to come home, get the boat, and go back for you—honest."

"What took you so long?"

"I got lost in the woods beyond the bog. But Fern was there with her cats, and she showed me how to get back to the trail by Murky Cove."

"*You* crossed the bog? With old lady Peet?" His eyes grew wide.

I stopped scratching Boogie, sat up perfectly straight, and looked down at my tennies. "That's right, and you won't believe what else happened." I told him all about Fern's strange picnic and borrowing her sweater, but I left out the part about the sacred ground and the green heron. Fern had asked me to keep that secret, and I couldn't betray her, not even to Jimmy.

"You'll have to take me there sometime, now that you know the way," he said.

Boogie grunted and rolled over on his back. I rubbed his fat belly while his feet stuck up in the air and his tongue hung out the side of his mouth in a silly grin.

"What are you going to do with the sweater?" There were tiny specks of brown in the blue of Jimmy's eyes. They must have been there all along, but I'd never noticed them before.

"I already returned it." The specks were so fascinating, changing from brown to blue to green.

"How could you? I mean, you're grounded, right?"

Lowering my voice to a whisper, I said, "I sneaked out and gave it back to her, just a little while ago."

"You did? Unbelievable!"

Leaning close to Jimmy, I rested my chin on his shoulder and whispered in his ear. As I told him about the chocolate cake and the piano lesson he kept nodding his head and saying, "Awesome!" When I finished, he turned his head, and his nose bumped mine. He was so close, it would have been easy for him to kiss me, maybe just an accidental brush like the last time in Smitty's backyard, but he didn't.

"Time to come in, Ronnie," Mom said from the other side of the screen. Jimmy and I sat back quickly.

"How about going swimming on Wednesday afternoon, the three of us? I only work mornings." Jimmy stood up and looked down at me.

"But Amy said she'd never speak to me again."

"Sure she will. I'll talk to her about it. The Clamdiggers can't stay mad at each other for long. See you then," he said. Waving, he called to Boogie and rode off.

# 11

# Snake-kissed Hair

*Wednesday morning my prison sentence was* up at last. After telling Mom I was going to Amy's, I took off for Fern's instead. I spent about an hour practicing "Twinkle, Twinkle" and "Tomcat Boogie." When I finished, Mrs. Peet gave me a cassette tape to take home.

"George took all my old records with him one day," she explained. "To copy them, in case they ever got broken. He gave me the tapes and a player for my birthday one year. Now you can hear me when I was really good."

Walking home for lunch, I realized I'd forgotten to get Mom's Cake Taker. Just the thought of my mom made me feel guilty. I hardly ever lied to her, and it seemed I was doing it a lot lately. I wanted to tell her all about Fern, how nice she really was, and how her son wanted to put her in a home, but I decided to wait for a while. Even though my mom was usually understanding, she had been very upset about that skiing incident. Right then, I couldn't stand the thought of having to give up the piano lessons. And Fern—she was turning out to be a real friend, not like some people I knew.

When I got to Jimmy's that afternoon, he was swimming in front of his house, and Amy was sunning herself on the dock. She looked the other way as soon as I got near.

Ignoring the snub, I sat beside her and watched Jimmy surface dive. Farther down the shoreline, on the old stone pier, I saw a single fisherman. "Amy, I'm sorry you thought I was dead," I began.

"Well, I should hope so!" she replied, turning toward me. It was then that I noticed the two blond streaks in her dark hair, one on each side of her face.

"What did you do to your hair?" I asked.

"It's sun-kissed. James likes it this way. I just used a little peroxide . . . but don't change the subject. I can't understand how you could do what you did to us." She wiggled away from me on the towel.

"I took a bad fall skiing barefoot, and I got mad

because you weren't spotting me." We both watched Jimmy, who was now swimming toward the dock on his back, water spurting from his mouth like a whale.

"Even if that's true, you didn't have to disappear. Where were you all that time?"

"Ronnie got lost in the bog, and met old lady Peet," Jimmy answered for me, pulling himself onto the dock.

"You were stuck in the bog with Mrs. Peet? Or shall I say your good friend, Fern."

"She was having some sort of picnic with her cats," I explained. "She lent me her sweater and showed me how to find my way back to the trail." Amy didn't seem too impressed, but at least we were talking to each other again.

"Yeah, and guess what else?" Jimmy said. He leaned on a piling with one elbow. "Ronnie baked her a cake, and went right over to her house and gave it to her. And Mrs. Peet gave Ronnie a piano lesson. Did you know the old catlady used to be a famous pianist?"

I wished Jimmy would keep his mouth shut. Amy didn't need to know everything, especially the part about my sneaking out while I was grounded. She didn't say a word, but I could see the wheels turning in her head. "Want to do some log-rolling?" I asked her.

"Naw, that's so childish. I'll sit here and get some more rays."

I looked at Jimmy. The water had slicked his hair back close to his head. That, and the sun glistening on his wet shoulders, made him look different somehow. I think I understood what Amy had been talking about when she said he was dreamy.

"I will," he volunteered, jumping into the water, cannonball style. Amy scowled and turned over onto her stomach. Had she always been such a drag?

Jimmy and I found a partly waterlogged tree trunk and rolled it in the water until it was near the dock. Then we stood on it, shifting our feet to balance. The point of log-rolling was to stay upright while making the other guy fall off.

"Take that," Jimmy said, bending over to splash me. "And that, and that, and that." He clung to the log with his feet, just like a monkey. I stole a glance at Amy and was happy to see her watching us. She was lying on her side, her elbow resting on a bent knee. I guessed she was daydreaming about being a model in a bathing suit ad.

"What's that swimming this way?" Jimmy asked, pointing away from shore. A moving ripple was coming toward us. "Maybe we can see better from the dock." We both climbed out of the water to check.

"Hey, it's Boogers! Here boy, here Boogers," Jimmy called. "I wonder where he's been all day. I haven't seen him since I fed him his supper last night."

"Probably catching lunch," I said. Boogie moved

through the water smoothly, his head and nose gliding on the surface.

"At least he doesn't have a dead fish to dump on us," Amy remarked.

Boogie heaved himself up on the dock and dropped a large, very much alive water snake on Amy's towel, where it froze, staring at her.

"*Eeeeeeeeyow!*" Amy screamed, diving into the water.

"Awesome!" Jimmy sidestepped the snake and tried to examine it.

I wasn't thrilled with Boogie's find like Jimmy was, but there was nothing to be afraid of. Northern water snakes aren't poisonous, and most of the time they just want to get away from you.

"Imagine Boogers being fast enough to catch a water snake!" he said proudly.

"Is it poisonous?" Amy asked from the water. Before Jimmy could answer, the snake slithered off the dock and landed on her shoulder.

"Water moccasin!" I yelled. "One bite and you're dead!" Of course, there weren't any water moccasins in Sandglass Lake, but I doubted if Amy knew that. Her arms and legs churned the water into froth as she frantically swam the few feet to shore. I laughed out loud. Jimmy laughed too, in a long string of ha-ha-hee-hees.

The shoreline on Jimmy's end of the island was

steep and rocky, and each time Amy tried to climb out of the water, she slipped on the wet moss and slid back in. Her sun-kissed hair was wet and stringy now. *Snake*-kissed hair was more like it. Black eye makeup ran down her cheeks, leaving two long streaks.

"James, James! Don't just stand there. Help me!" she cried angrily.

Jimmy went to the rescue. He pulled her out of the water, wrapping her in his towel.

"Did it bite me?" she asked, pushing the towel away.

Jimmy ran his hand over her shoulders and back. "Naw, you're all right. And besides, we don't have any water moccasins around here."

Amy buried her face in the terry cloth and tried to wipe off the runny mascara. She glared at me over the top of the towel.

I was ready. "Are you sure about that, Jimmy?" I said. Then I gave her my sweetest smile.

# 12

# Tattletale

*Mom made strawberry shortcake for dessert* that night. After the dishes were cleared, Dad and I watched her spoon mashed berries over the homemade biscuits.

"Looks delicious, Kathy," Dad said. He was reaching across the kitchen table for the whipped topping when Jimmy and Amy knocked on the screen. Mom invited them in to join us.

"Thanks, Mrs. Windslow," Jimmy said, grabbing an extra chair. He loved strawberry shortcake like Boogie loved dead carp. But Amy sat down faster, next to me. Jimmy ended up between her and my dad.

We were all eating when Mom said, "I was going to send your parents some biscuits, Amy, but I can't find my Cake Taker. Have you seen it, Ronnie?"

I shook my head no. It was hard not to wince—I knew what was coming.

"She probably left it over at her friend Mrs. Peet's house," Amy said.

"Mrs. Peet's house? Whatever gave you that idea, Amy?" Mom looked at me, her gray eyes growing suspicious.

I desperately tried to think of something to say.

"Oh, I'm sorry," Amy gushed, wiping her lips daintily with a napkin. "I didn't mean . . . I just assumed you knew . . . I . . . oh, how embarrassing."

"Assumed I knew what?" Mom asked.

"Well," Amy stammered, and blinked. She was really laying it on now. "I thought you knew, especially since Ronnie is taking piano lessons from her."

"Piano lessons? From old Mrs. Peet?" My mother balanced on her elbows and leaned across the table, her eyes searching my face.

"I'm so sorry, Ronnie. I didn't mean to cause any trouble," Amy murmured. She put her hand on my shoulder, then turned to Jimmy, who was busy scraping every bit of whipped cream from his plate. "I think we had better go now, James," she said. I almost clapped.

"Just a sec." Jimmy fingered the last bit of topping from the sides of the bowl. Pushing back his chair, he asked, "You coming, Ronnie?"

I doubted he had heard a word of our conversation but I stood up, glad at the chance to escape.

"Wait just a minute." Mom's voice was a warning. "What's all this nonsense about taking piano lessons from Mrs. Peet?"

Looking into my mother's steel gray eyes, I said, "It was just one little lesson."

"I think you two had better go on without Ronnie for now," Mom said evenly. "We have some things to discuss."

"Uh . . . okay," Jimmy stammered, and he and Amy escaped out the door. I sighed and sat back down.

"You mean you really are taking piano lessons from Mrs. Peet?" Mom asked. She waited. Dad stopped eating. They were interested in the answer I was going to give. So was I, desperately.

"How do you even know Mrs. Peet?" Dad asked.

"And what does she have to do with my missing Cake Taker?" I was sure being grounded for one week was nothing compared to what I'd get now.

"Tell us everything," Mom urged.

I did. I had to. "That day when I got lost in the woods, I never would have gotten home if Fern hadn't helped me."

"Fern? You mean Mrs. Peet, don't you," Mom corrected me.

"She asked me to call her Fern. She was there on a picnic, and she knows how to get through the bog. It was her sweater I was wearing when I came home. She gave it to me because I was cold."

"Why didn't you tell me about the sweater then? And what does this have to do with my Cake Taker?"

"And the piano lessons," Dad added.

"I didn't tell you about the sweater, because I know how you feel about Fern, and you were mad enough already. And remember the day I baked the cake? I was thinking about Fern and how she always wears that sweater, and maybe needed it back. So I baked her a cake, too, and took it to her house. She showed me her piano and played it for me. I couldn't believe how good she was. She told me how she used to be a concert pianist, but had to give it up because of arthritis."

Mom sat back in her chair and I slumped down in mine, trying to disappear. I'm really going to get it now, I thought, but it felt good to tell the truth.

"You went down to Mrs. Peet's while you were grounded?" Mom kept boring in.

"Mrs. Peet used to be a concert pianist?" Dad asked.

I took the out. "That's right," I said eagerly. "She even gave me some of her recordings so I could hear her when she was real good. Wait—I'll show you." I ran to my room and returned with the cassette tape.

" 'Beethoven's Sonatas by Fern Meinhart,' " Dad read aloud from the label. "Fern Meinhart? I haven't heard of her in ages." He handed the tape back to me. "You mean Mrs. Peet down the road is Fern Meinhart, the pianist?"

I nodded my head and told them about my piano lessons. "She said I could learn to play, too, if I worked hard at it. She said I have good hands and a talent for music."

"I used to love to listen to her music." Dad flipped the tape over on the table. "I didn't know she was from around here, though."

"She moved here after she quit playing," I explained.

"I know you like classical music," Mom said to Dad. "But I don't remember any Fern Meinhart."

"Back when I was at the police academy, there was this one instructor who was determined to teach us culture along with criminology," Dad explained. "Fern Meinhart was an obsession of his and he used to play these old records of hers in class. She was quite a genius."

The discussion was going better than I'd hoped. They even seemed to have forgotten about my sneaking out. "She's already taught me two songs," I said. "Just watch." Placing my hands on the table, I sang and fake-played "Twinkle, Twinkle."

"Well, I'm not so sure," Mom said. "We don't know her, and she is pretty eccentric. In all the years we've lived on Harbor Island, I've only seen her a few times. Recently, Martha Jackman said good morning to her in the supermarket. Mrs. Peet just looked right through Martha like she wasn't even there."

"But what about the piano lessons?"

"They say all great artists are a bit eccentric," Dad put in.

"Fern's real nice, just lonesome," I explained. "That's why she has all those cats. Please, please can I take piano lessons? It's something I *have* to do."

Dad put his hand over Mom's. "Just think, Kathy. Ronnie has a chance to study with a great artist. It's a rare opportunity."

I looked at Mom and nodded my head eagerly.

"Well, I'd sure like to see her learn music, but we don't even have a piano."

"I'm going to practice on hers."

"Wait a minute," Mom said thoughtfully. "It seems like that would be a big inconvenience for Mrs. Peet."

"I'm sure it isn't, Mom. Fern said she wants me to and she's expecting me to come every morning for an hour."

"Well, I suppose," Mom conceded. "But tell her we

101

are going to pay for the lessons, and if you do well and stay interested, maybe we could get a piano for Christmas."

"Thanks, Mom!" I jumped out of my chair and gave her a hug. Amy had tried her best to get me into trouble and it had backfired. I was taking piano lessons from Fern, and of course, Jimmy would be impressed with that.

"Don't think we've forgotten about your sneaking off while you were grounded," Mom added.

"I should have told you about Fern." It was my turn to concede.

"I agree," Mom said, and Dad nodded his head. "But we're going to let it go this time as long as you promise not to keep things like this from us anymore. Part of growing up is being responsible for your behavior, and being honest with us."

When it got right down to it, I had to admit my mom and dad were pretty nice. I wondered why I had ever lied to them in the first place. Of course, I hadn't told them yet about the visit from George. I was still worried Mom might think something was wrong with Fern, especially if they knew her son wanted to put her away. Besides, Fern said she and her son always argued whenever he came to visit. Then there was the mystery of the missing money. I was dying to know what happened to it.

# 13

# Mr. George Peet Returns

*The next morning I* listened to the Beethoven sonata tape on my Walkman, all through breakfast. Fern was right when she said she played much better back then. There were places where the music raced at such a furious pace, it was hard to imagine human hands moving over the keys that fast. I was still plugged in when I grabbed my piano music and some leftover shortcakes (Mom's idea), and headed for Fern's to practice.

As soon as I set foot on Beach Road, I saw Amy in front of Smitty's, walking toward my house. She jogged to meet me.

"Where are you going?" she asked, eyeing my sheet music.

I turned up the volume on my Walkman and yelled back, "I can't hear you!"

This time Amy pulled one earphone away from my head and screamed right into my ear, *"Where are you going?"*

"To Fern's to practice." I turned off my Walkman and jammed it into my pocket.

"You mean your mom's going to let you go on seeing old lady Peet?"

"Yes, and thanks for your help, Amy," I said, trying to sound sincere. "I didn't know how to tell Mom and Dad about Fern and the piano lessons. But it's okay. They think it's a great idea." I thought she looked disappointed.

"If I do well, Mom said I could even get my own piano for Christmas," I explained.

"Jeez, I can think of a lot more exciting things than a piano," she mumbled, looking down at her feet.

"Where were you going, anyway?" I asked.

"To your house. I was afraid you'd be grounded again, after I let it slip about Mrs. Peet in front of your folks."

"That was no accident, Amy Parrish, and you know it."

She scuffed her pink running shoes in the dust and

glanced sideways at me. "I feel just awful about that, honest."

For a second there, I saw the old Amy and believed she really was sorry. "Things turned out all right anyway." I smiled. "Where did you and Jimmy go after my house last night?"

She straightened her shoulders and looked away. "We walked up to Hadley's and messed around."

"Messed around doing what?"

"Actually, it was sort of like a date," she said. The old Amy had disappeared. "We sat on a picnic table under the willow trees and talked about, well, about private things, and . . ."

"And what?"

"And, that's all I'm telling. The rest is just between James and me, but it was very romantic."

Getting her to tell me more would be harder than getting Boogie to turn down a steak. Still I wondered, Did he hold her hand, put his arm around her, give her one of those accidental kisses? I decided not to forgive her after all.

Fern seemed pleased with the shortcakes, but she refused to take any money for the lessons.

"I'm teaching you about the piano because I want to," she said emphatically. "What good is being a genius if you can't pass some of it along?"

"My dad said you are a genius, but Mom said you're eccentric." The last word popped out before I could stop it.

We were sitting side by side on the piano bench. Fern held her head high and I could see the side of her long, straight nose. Looking at me out of the corner of her eye, she said, "I am not eccentric." Then, breaking into a smile, she added, "I'm unbalanced— and a genius!"

I laughed and woke Toothless up from his nap on top of the piano. After a long stretch, he hopped into Fern's lap. She stroked him on the back, her face becoming serious.

"I was born understanding music and was drawn to the piano with a passion. To develop that talent and passion took all my time. I thought nothing of sitting at the piano six hours a day." Toothless purred loudly and leaned his ear against her hand. "Math, English, or science didn't make any sense to me, just music. When I was your age, I didn't have any friends. The music and piano were enough." She scratched the old cat's ear.

"Sometimes I think it's easier not to have any friends," I said.

"Oh? Are you having trouble with those two pals of yours?"

"Amy has been my best friend forever, but she's changed, and now we're always at each other's throats."

"And does that young man have anything to do with it?"

I practiced a scale with my left hand. "Jimmy still likes me, or at least he does when we're alone. But he seems to like Amy better all the time. He thinks she's beautiful, and she is." I hit a wrong note and stopped.

Fern placed my third finger on F-sharp. "Amy is very pretty, and young boys are always attracted to good looks. However, you're pretty, too, Veronica, and have a lot more to offer besides."

"Maybe . . ."

"I've seen the three of you around the island several times lately. Even these old eyes of mine couldn't help but notice that Amy's kind of unbalanced herself right now. As soon as her newness starts to wear off, Jimmy will pay attention to you, too. The three of you will be good friends again, but in a different way." She squeezed my shoulder. "Remember this, Veronica. It's better to be well-rounded than unbalanced."

"I'll remember," I promised. Across the cover of my practice book Fern had written, "Veronica's Notebook." I turned to the new piece she had written, "Waltz of the Green Heron," and haltingly played the right hand.

"Sit up straight and count out loud," Fern commanded.

"One, two, three," we said together.

A loud knocking on the front door interrupted my

107

music. The sound made Toothless jump out of Fern's lap. Before anyone could answer the door, Mr. Peet walked in. "Mother . . . I . . . oh! I didn't realize you had company."

"Let me introduce you to my friend and student, Veronica," Fern said. "Veronica, this is my son, George, or at least he used to be."

"Please, Mother, don't start as soon as I get here." He went to the kitchen, came out with a chair, and sat down next to the piano. "I'm pleased to meet you, Veronica. Student? You don't mean you're teaching piano?"

"Yes, and Veronica is very talented, too."

George looked at me and said, "I don't mean to be rude, but I really must talk to my mother alone."

"It's all right." I felt very awkward. "It's time to go anyway."

"Stay where you are," Fern demanded. She put her hand across my lap. "I want a witness."

"Mother, please." Turning toward me, George said, "You'd really better go. She might make a scene."

"I'm not leaving," I replied solemnly. Refusing to obey an adult made me feel guilty. But I was sure Fern had her reasons for wanting me to stay.

"Have it your own way." Mr. Peet shrugged and scooted his chair closer to Fern. "Mother," he began. "It worries me to think of you living all alone out here. What if you fell down and broke a leg, or had a heart attack?" His voice was soft and he seemed to really care about his mother. "Let me tell you about the really nice place I found called Maple Hills. It's only a mile from my house. They offer meals in the dining room, maid service, an emergency buzzer in every room and . . ."

"What? *What!*" she shrieked, spinning around to face the piano and playing several loud, haunting chords.

"There's no need to get upset, Mother." George reached over, took Fern's hands off the keys, and held them gently. "I only want to help you."

"You're an ungrateful son of a pup!" she replied, pulling her hands away and rubbing them together. "That's what you are. You found out what I did with the money and now you want to punish me."

"As for the money . . ." George paused and looked over at me. "I think we'd better discuss that later. And I don't want to punish you—just take care of you. Since you refuse to consider moving to Maple Hills, will you at least call Dr. Burke in Northwood and get a checkup?"

"Didn't I read in the paper a year or so ago that he had retired?" Fern said matter-of-factly.

George's red, round face grew serious. "I had no idea you weren't seeing Dr. Burke anymore," he said thoughtfully. "Maple Hills has excellent medical care. The doctors there could—"

"Get out!" Fern jumped to her feet. "And don't ever mention that place to me again."

"I'm going," Mr. Peet said, standing up. Bending down, he kissed her on the top of the head. "I'd hoped we could talk about this together and come to a reasonable decision about what's best for you, but I can see that's impossible." He crossed the room and stopped by the front door. "I'll be back as soon as I decide what to do next," he said, and left.

I couldn't figure it out. Mr. Peet acted like he truly loved his mother, yet Fern seemed to hate him. But if he loved her, why didn't he understand how important it was to her to stay on the island?

"What's best is for him to stay out of my business," Fern mumbled. Then, turning to me, she smiled. "Start playing from measure twelve." We finished the lesson as if George hadn't come at all.

# 14

# Murder

*The Fourth of July weekend arrived, along* with the usual rush of holiday boaters. On the night of the fourth, Mom and I went to Jimmy's house to see the fireworks. (Dad was across the lake on the barge at Mallard's Landing, helping the Northwood Kiwanis Club launch the Roman candles and rockets.) I watched the entire show with Mom, Mr. and Mrs. Parrish, and Mr. and Mrs. Jackman. Just before it started, Amy persuaded Jimmy to walk her home to get her sweater, and they didn't return until an hour and a half later.

The rest of the month was about as eventful. Still banned from waterskiing by my dad, Jimmy continued to work mornings at Hadley's, and Amy usually stayed in until noon. Most afternoons we all met at the marina and whiled away the hours fishing off the bridge. Although I had given up hope of catching another bass for the contest, Fern was always delighted to get whatever I caught. On the plus side, piano lessons were going smoothly, and Mr. Peet hadn't been back.

I was on my way to the bridge on the last day of July when I found Boogie sitting at my front door, wagging his tail.

"What are you doing here, boy, looking for lunch?" He answered by offering me his paw. I took it and scratched him under the chin. Then I got my bike out of the garage and hung my minnow net and bucket on the handlebar. Boogie followed and watched.

"Well, come on, let's go see Jimmy," I called, pedaling out into the road. Boogie took off and briefly ran beside me. But by the time I got in front of Fern's, he was falling behind and starting to pant.

"Come on, Boogie," I encouraged him, slapping my leg. "You need the exercise."

Instead of trotting closer to my bike, he darted into the woods across the road from Fern's. Almost immediately Toothless shot out of the brush and ran in front of me, Boogie on his tail. I skidded to a stop and managed to save the minnow bucket from spilling. The cat streaked across Fern's yard.

"*No, no!* Boogie, *come!*" I shouted, but it was no

use. He caught the cat in the middle of the tall grass. Twisting and tumbling, they became one yellow and gray fur-ball.

"Stop it right *now!*" I demanded. I got off my bike and chased after them. Toothless raced out of the long weeds and headed for the oak tree with Boogie close behind. As the cat jumped up the tree, Boogie stopped so fast he bonked his head on the trunk.

Since Toothless seemed to have escaped, I stopped running. But there was more. The old cat walked out onto a lower branch over Boogie's head, arched his back, and hissed at the dog. Boogie responded with an astonishing bound straight up. With his front paws, he caught the branch below Toothless and pulled it toward the ground. As he fell, the branch sprung upward and hit Toothless's perch. The smack must have caught the old cat by surprise.

*Whompf!* He tumbled out of the tree and hit the ground with a sickening thud. I ran for him, but Boogie was there first and scooped Toothless up in his mouth. Head up, tail wagging, he brought me his prize. The cat was limp, his head and front paws hung from one side of the dog's muzzle, hind legs and tail from the other.

"Good dog, bring me the kitty." I knew if I yelled, Boogie would run away and I'd never see Toothless again.

Boogie stood quietly while I pried his mouth open

and laid the cat gently on the ground. Then, grabbing him by the scruff of the neck, I shook Boogie furiously and shrieked, "Bad dog! Ugly mutt! Get out of here! I hate you!"

He yelped, struggled out of my grasp, and slunk off into the woods.

I stroked Toothless, and a big clump of hair fell out where Boogie had carried him. There were puncture marks on his skin. His eyes were glassy, and his chest was still.

A door slammed and I looked up to see Fern walking toward me. I scrambled to my feet, stepping in front of Toothless.

"What's the matter, Veronica? Fall off your bike? I heard you hollering clear in my house."

"No, I'm all right."

"Then what are you hiding there?" she asked, peering behind me.

What was Fern going to do without Toothless? He was her precious baby. I leaned back on my heels. "Nothing," I muttered, feeling completely helpless.

"Nonsense! I know when someone is hiding something from me. What kind of fish do you have today? Crappies? The family would love some baked crappies."

I gave up and stepped aside. A long, low whine came from Fern as she scooped Toothless up in her arms.

114

"Mama's poor, old, decrepit baby." She rocked him and pressed her face into his fur, then carried him back to the house. Before opening the door she turned and said, "Well, don't just stand there. Come on in, Veronica."

In the living room, she laid Toothless on the Oriental rug, in the spot where the concert grand used to stand. Tomcat crawled out from under the sofa and sniffed the body. He was soon joined by Birdy, Uncle Newt, and Cousin Jake.

"Come, family, and say good-bye to Toothless." Fern took my arm, and slowly, painfully, lowered herself to the floor by the dead cat. We watched the family gather around. Fern touched the end of Toothless's nose with her finger. "Poor, dead kitty. He was so old and arthritic, just like me. Now he doesn't hurt anymore, but I sure will miss him." She looked at me, her fingers picking at the buttons on her dress. "How did this happen?"

I sat on the floor beside her. "Boogie, Jimmy's dog, chased Toothless and caught him. They had a big fight and Toothless ran up a tree. Boogie jumped and shook the branch where Toothless was sitting, and he fell out. By the time I got him away from Boogie, he was dead. I'm not sure which killed him—the fall or Boogie."

I felt Tomcat rubbing against me and picked him up. He felt so warm and alive. "I'm sorry, Fern," I said. How I wished I could have been faster.

115

"It wasn't your fault, Veronica." The button she had been twisting came off in her hand.

"It was all Boogie's fault. He's a murderer, and I hate him!"

"He's not a murderer; he's a dog. Not so different than Birdy, really. She kills birds. I don't like it—but it's just something she does."

"But why? Why does Boogie have to kill things?" I pulled Tomcat's front paws up on my shoulder and let him stroke my cheek.

"Usually animals kill to eat, but sometimes, like Birdy and Boogie, the instinct to hunt is very strong. I just wish he hadn't hunted poor, old Toothless." Tucking the button in her pocket, she rubbed her hands together, then clapped them once. "Well, no matter how it happened, the deed is done and there's only one thing to do now."

"What's that?"

"We'll have a funeral, of course. To help us say good-bye. Now help me up. We have a lot of work to do."

Fern led me through the kitchen and down a narrow hallway into her bedroom. In it was a double bed with tall posters at the corners and a yellowed lace canopy on top. The bed was covered by an ancient-looking quilt where several ragged, stuffed toy cats sat.

She opened the door of the closet, which seemed to contain old clothes and a collection of fabric swatches.

116

One hanger held long strips of blue velvet. Yellow satin hung over another. Fern sorted through a long black evening dress covered with sequins, a lacy black shawl, a short brown jacket and apron, and stopped at a single piece of rose-colored material.

"I was saving this for the occasion," she explained. "Only Toothless can have the last scrap." Taking the rose fabric from the hanger, she handed it to me.

It felt soft and silky, like wedding dress material. One edge was folded and had tiny holes in it. The other edge had been cut with a scissors. Fern and I went into the kitchen where she spread the fabric onto the table. "Bring Toothless over here, and put him on his shroud," she said to me.

"What's a shroud?" I was beginning to feel uncomfortable.

"A burial cloth for the dead."

So she wasn't kidding about the funeral. With my fingertips I carefully felt the fur of the dead cat. Cupping my hands under him, I noticed he was starting to get stiff. He would lie forever on his side, I thought, with his legs sticking out as if he were walking. I swallowed hard, to keep from gagging.

Fern took Toothless from me, cuddled him against her neck, and kissed him on the ear. Gently, she laid him on top of the material and wrapped it around him like a baby blanket.

"Special fabric for a special cat," she murmured.

Then suddenly, she grabbed a corner and pulled the material out from under him. Holding it next to her face, she smiled and said, "Johan Pabst, the artist who painted my portrait, said this was my best color. What do you think?"

The rosy remnant made her face look pasty white, and her light eyes almost colorless.

"Very nice," I lied.

"Oh, come on, Veronica," she said, waving the scrap in the air. "It's a young girl's color. Once it was part of my favorite concert gown, but now . . ." Fern's face went blank. She dropped the shroud on top of the cat, put her hand to her head, and sank into a chair.

"Are you all right?" I leaned over and put my arm around her.

"Just give me a minute and it will pass." The words came slowly. "It always does." Fern took my hand in hers and turned it over. "You seem so far away, and your face is all blurry."

"I'd better call my mom or something."

"No, no." She shook her head and pulled herself up straighter in the chair. "I get these dizzy spells sometimes and then they go away. In fact, I'm fine now, except for a little headache. Funerals always give me a headache."

"Can I get you something?"

"Yes, you can get me some mourners. I want

118

Toothless to go out in style." Fern squeezed my hand and cocked her head to one side.

"Mourners?"

"Of course. We're going to make this the best funeral any of my family ever had. Go and get those two friends of yours, especially that young man. He's surely strong enough to dig a good, deep grave."

# 15

# The Sacred Ground

*I met Amy and Jimmy walking up the road* from the marina. They were looking for me since I hadn't shown up to fish.

"You want us to do *what*?" Amy snapped.

"Go to a funeral for Toothless," I repeated, trying to make it sound normal.

Amy looked at Jimmy, her mouth in an O, and she shook her head as if to say, "No way."

"A funeral for a cat? Outstanding!" Jimmy missed Amy's message.

"It's the least you can do, Jimmy Jackman," I said, poking him in the stomach with my finger. "It was your dog that killed him."

"Aw, Boogers has been chasing those cats for years, never even touched one."

"Well, he caught one this time, because I saw the whole thing."

Jimmy looked shocked. He hung his head and scuffed the dirt with his feet. "I bet Mrs. Peet wouldn't want me there. Not after Boogie . . ."

"Oh yes, she does. She said she needs you to dig the grave, and you don't have to be afraid of her. She isn't mad about Boogie, but I am."

"Afraid? I'm not afraid of Mrs. Peet," he said, squaring his shoulders. "We'd better go, Amy. Mrs. Peet needs our help."

I opened Fern's front door. Jimmy followed me, dragging Amy behind him. We found Fern sitting at the piano wearing the black dress I had seen in her closet. It was covered in shiny sequins except for a few bare patches where they had fallen off. Amy stared at the holey tennies sticking out from under the hem.

"Oh, I see the mourners are here," Fern welcomed us. "Now I can start." She turned to the keyboard and played: "DUM DUM daDUM. DUM DUM daDUM." The heavy bass notes boomed from the piano. Apparently, this was one of the days when Fern's arthritis let up a little—or maybe the memory of Toothless prodded her on.

I'd heard the somber music she played before, in

121

cartoons, but it wasn't funny now. The bass notes kept thumping sadly, and were soon joined by a minor melody from the high notes. I watched Amy put her hand on Jimmy's shoulder. Then, motionless, we all listened, as the dark, powerful sound surrounded us.

"Chopin could write a dandy funeral march," Fern said when she had finished. A hairpin had fallen out in the middle of the piece and, with white frizz hanging over one side of her face, she looked wilder than ever.

"Fern, I'd like you to meet my friends, Amy and Jimmy."

"Delighted, I'm sure," she said, scrutinizing them carefully. "I don't suppose your mothers ever taught you to wear black to a funeral, but never mind, I'll fix that." We watched her walk through the kitchen, and disappear in the hall to her bedroom.

"Did you check out that dress? And that was the creepiest music I've ever heard!" Jimmy said in a loud whisper.

"It made my skin crawl," Amy whispered back. "And what's that?" She pointed to the lumpy sack on the kitchen table, just as Fern returned with her arms full.

"The deceased, of course," she answered matter-of-factly. "Here's something for you, Veronica." Fern threw a black shawl over my shoulders that smelled worse than her sweater. "Your black trousers will do for you, sir," she said, nodding at Jimmy's gym shorts.

Finally, on tiptoe, Fern draped a square of black lace over Amy's sun-kissed hair. I enjoyed seeing her squirm.

"You, sir." Fern pointed to Jimmy. "There's a shovel in the garage. Would you get it for me, and oh yes, please dig up a small clump of catnip—there's a patch of it right behind the garage. Be sure you get the roots, too."

"Uh, I guess I could do that," Jimmy muttered, and left. A few minutes later he came back with a big green clump.

Fern handed the catnip to me, picked up Toothless, and said, "Now we're ready to visit the sacred ground."

"But Fern." I leaned close to her and whispered. "What about keeping the sacred ground a secret?"

"It's okay, Veronica," she answered out loud. "I want a big funeral for Toothless. And besides, the time for secrets is running out."

We made a strange procession walking through the woods. Fern, in her black sequins, led the way, clutching the dead cat to her chest. I followed with Amy behind me (looking very dramatic with her black lace cap), and Jimmy at the rear, carrying the shovel. Tomcat trotted at my heel, and the rest of the family found their own way through the underbrush. No one spoke until Fern led us off the trail near the cove, into the bog.

"We can't go in there," Amy hissed. "We'll get stuck!"

Looking over my shoulder, I saw that she had stopped cold. Jimmy poked her in the back and said, "Get moving, Amy." She moved.

Wordlessly, we followed Fern's careful steps across the mucky ground and into the woods on the opposite side. As soon as we reached the clearing where she and I had sat on the day of the waterskiing incident, she stopped. Then, standing at the end of a row of catnip clumps, she signalled to Jimmy. "Dig here." With the toe of her sneaker, she pointed to the spot.

The ground was soft, and Jimmy quickly dug a deep hole. When he was finished, he leaned against the handle of the shovel, one foot resting on the blade.

"I think we should say something over the grave," Fern said crisply. Aunt Hester and Uncle Jake sat at her feet, and Birdy pawed at the sequins near the hem of her dress. Staring at Jimmy she said, "Would you like to do the eulogy?"

"I . . . well . . . I guess I could," he answered, taking his foot off the shovel and standing up straight. With a serious expression on his face, he began. "We are here today to bury this good and faithful cat, Toothless." Jimmy paused and looked at Amy and me for help.

"We will all miss him," Amy said quickly.

"May he rest in peace," I added.

Fern gave a slight sniffle and rubbed her eyes. "That was lovely, just lovely," she said, looking up. Then her pale face brightened slightly. "Look." Toothless in one hand, she pointed to the top of a pine with the other. "The Woods Brothers came to pay their respects." I followed her glance and saw three large brown and black cats perched among the branches.

Suddenly, Fern began to wobble, then to sway back and forth. As Toothless slid from her arm and landed in the grave with a thud, Jimmy and I grabbed the old woman by the arms and let her gently sink to the ground. There she sat, staring into the hole. "Oh my, Toothless! I didn't mean . . ."

I knelt beside her and whispered, "Maybe we should go home now." Tomcat poked my arm with his nose.

Raising her hand in protest, Fern said, "I'll be okay. Let's get on with it." She pointed at the shovel, and Jimmy went to work, filling the hole.

"Ronnie. Pssst, Ronnie!" Amy hissed.

"What is it?" I stood up next to her.

"Get it away from me—now!" "It" was Brother Blackie, who was rubbing his head up and down on her leg. I shooed him away while Jimmy planted the clump of catnip and tramped the dirt down around it.

"Good-bye Toothless, Mama's precious little kitty," Fern chanted.

"Miaoooow!" Aunt Hester wailed, crawling into

Fern's lap. The cat's hair stood on end In the silence that followed, we heard something moving behind a fallen tree. Then we saw a flash of yellow, and Boogie's head appeared.

"You cat killer—I'm going to get you now!" I threatened, but Boogie bounded off into the woods before I could catch him.

"Veronica, that's not the way," Fern scolded.

"But he killed Toothless. He's always killing other animals."

"He doesn't mean to, honest," Jimmy protested, his mouth small and tight. He rubbed his shoe against the newly planted catnip, and went on, "I'm real sorry for what he did to Toothless."

"It's okay, Jimmy," Fern said. "Boogie is only a beast of nature, a hunter. It was time for Toothless to go, and when it's your time, I don't think how it happens is that important." She pushed Aunt Hester from her lap and reached for Jimmy's hand. He took hers and helped her to her feet.

"Thank you all for coming to the funeral. Toothless would have liked it. Actually, *he* doesn't care a whit one way or the other. Funerals are for the living. They don't do a thing for the dead." Fern started walking off toward the bog, so Jimmy grabbed the shovel and we all went after her. Suddenly, she stopped and leaned against a tree trunk.

126

"Are you dizzy again?" I asked, hurrying up behind her.

"No, just a headache. Funerals always give me a headache."

"Here." Jimmy offered her his arm, which Fern accepted, and together they continued slowly on. Amy and I trailed them, dodging the cats who cut back and forth along our path.

At her door, Fern smiled weakly. "Thank you once more for coming. It was the best funeral I've been to in a long time."

"I'm sorry about Boogers," Jimmy apologized again.

She patted his arm. "I understand."

There was a long silence. Finally, Amy said, "I have to go home . . . er . . . my mother must want me for something." She handed Fern the lacy square from her head. I wondered, What she was thinking about my eccentric friend now?

"I'll put the shovel away," Jimmy volunteered. He went around the side of the garage, followed by Amy.

"Can I come in and stay with you awhile?" I asked. I was really nervous about those dizzy spells.

"Don't worry about me, Veronica." Fern squeezed my arm. "I want to be alone now, but be sure and come for your lesson in the morning." She took the shawl from my shoulders, and shut the door.

As I turned to leave, Jimmy and Amy returned from

the garage. "Imagine that!" Jimmy was saying. "A graveyard for cats beyond the bog. And she wasn't even mad about Boogers."

Amy fell into step beside me. "Ronnie, how can you be friends with such a person?" she asked. "That woman has a screw loose somewhere. That music, and her dress, and a dead cat in a bag! I feel like I just visited the 'Twilight Zone.' " She pulled her hair forward over her eyes and began to pick through it. "It's a wonder I don't have lice from that awful thing I had to wear."

"She may be a little strange," Jimmy said. "But there's something about her I can't quite describe. . . ."

"Probably her smell. It was pretty indescribable," Amy complained, shaking her head. "Come, James." She took his hand. "I have to go home and shampoo my hair. You can wait for me on the porch."

"I guess we're not going fishing," Jimmy moaned. But he let himself be dragged off all the same.

I thought of Fern, cuddling Toothless against her face and calling him her precious kitty. He was her favorite, and I felt sorry for her. The funny thing was she didn't blame Boogie and she didn't seem to feel sorry for herself either. It was his time to go, and she just accepted that he was gone.

# 16

# Moonlight Concert

*That night, after supper, I agreed to do the* dishes so Mom and Dad could go for a ride in the Chris Craft before dark. While I was drying the glasses, the phone rang. It was Amy. She and "James" were "going out," she said, so they would see me tomorrow. I hung up and shined the silverware one piece at a time.

After that, I tried watching a movie on TV, but it was a romance, and every time the boy kissed the girl, I thought about Jimmy and Amy. Flipping the channels, I found a wildlife show about tigers. But that reminded me of poor, dead Toothless, and Fern, sitting at home alone, missing him.

The kitchen door slammed. "We're back," Mom

129

called. I could hear her rustling for ice cubes. "What are you watching?"

"Nothing very interesting," I said, turning off the set. "I think I'll go over to Amy's for a while to play cards or something." Of course, I had no intention of getting near Amy and Jimmy, but I wanted to get out of the house without a lot of questions.

"Okay, but it's already eight-thirty and I want you in by ten," Mom said firmly.

"No problem." I held up my wrist so she could see I had on my watch.

Sandglass was choppy, and the warm breeze smelled like flowers. Taking off my shoes, I waded around Smitty's fences and stopped on Fern's beach. I wanted to peek in the window to see if she was all right, but the sudden sound of piano music stopped me. I recognized the funeral march Fern had played earlier for Toothless. Sitting under the willow tree, I put my shoes beside me in the long, weedy grass. I wrapped my arms around my knees, and listened. When the piece was over, Fern moved on to another somber melody, then another.

In the moonlight, I tried to imagine Fern as she looked in her portrait, on stage and playing to a theater full of people. Then I saw Jimmy's silhouette, walking down the beach toward me. I looked at my watch. It was a couple of minutes before ten. Halfway across Fern's backyard, Jimmy stopped, then crept slowly toward the open window.

"Pssst!" I whispered. He spotted me and crawled over.

"What are you doing here?" he demanded, plopping down next to me.

"I might ask you the same thing. Why were you sneaking up on Fern?"

"I was just walking by and heard the music."

"You wanted to see if she was all right, you mean."

"Well, yeah." He stretched out in the long weeds. "She did seem sort of sick today, but it sounds like she's okay now." I was proud of Jimmy for worrying about Fern, too.

Abruptly, the funeral music stopped, leaving only the sound of the waves splashing. Then came a series of loud, crashing chords, followed by an echo of softer notes. It was the beginning of a sonata— one I'd heard before, on Fern's tape, and played far, far better. Still, it was beautiful. The high notes were so sharp, they sounded like she was plucking the strings of a harp.

"That's fantastic!" Jimmy said.

"I know," I agreed.

I laid back in the grass next to Jimmy, and we looked up at the sky. Thousands of stars shone and winked. Jimmy rolled over onto his side, propped his head on his hand, and stared into my eyes. "I can see why you want to play like her. Do you think you ever will?"

"Probably not that well," I said softly, "but I'm sure going to try." Maybe it was the music but it seemed to me that Jimmy's hair was pure gold in the moonlight, and his eyes were absolutely dazzling.

"I can see the stars in your eyes," he whispered.

My mind raced. "Where's Amy?" I stammered, immediately embarrassed. Of all times to remind him of Amy!

"She had to be in by ten." He closed his eyes and leaned so close that our lips were only an inch apart.

Right then, I didn't care that it was probably after ten. Was Jimmy going to kiss me or not? And if he was, what was he waiting for? And what would it feel like this time? Fern's music raced at a frantic pace, and Jimmy pressed his lips against mine. To my surprise, I felt myself closing my eyes, too, and pressing back. After a couple of seconds I felt sort of silly, my lips stuck to his, but neither of us seemed to know what to do.

So I made the next move. Pulling away, I said, "I was supposed to be in by ten."

"Okay." He sat up and combed his hair with his fingers. "Remember our sentence is up tomorrow—August the first. Meet me at Amy's around twelve-thirty to go skiing." Then he hopped up and cut through the side of Fern's yard, heading for the road.

Shoes in hand, I strolled along the beach, thinking about what had just happened. Sandglass looked so beautiful, with the moon, a huge yellow ball, hanging low, over the sparkling water. It was an honest-to-goodness kiss, I decided, not an iffy one like the other time. "Clamdiggers forever," I whispered, then laughed out loud.

# 17

# Wedding Present

*Sit up straighter, Veronica!"* Fern commanded. "And count out loud. One ah, two ah, three ah, four!" She rapped my shoulder with her knuckles on each beat. It was nine o'clock the next morning and I had showed up for my practice session with four small crappies for the family. Fern said nothing about Toothless or the funeral—she was eager to get right to work.

"No, no, that will never do," she said sternly. "You'd better stop and start all over again. Maybe you're not ready for eighth notes yet."

I started again, but the new sonatina was hard.

"A little slower, please," she interrupted.

Dropping my hands in my lap, I sighed. "Why can't I play the whole thing and then worry about the mistakes?"

"Because you should never let a mistake get by you," Fern replied. "You've got to fix them up before going on to the next one, and Veronica, there will always be a next one."

"One ah, two ah, three ah, four." I started over, and over again, before I made it all the way to the end.

"You deserve a break after that." Fern relaxed a bit. "Can I get you some tea?"

"No thanks, I'm not thirsty." I had tasted her tea once before.

"Me either." She eased herself onto the couch and patted the cushion next to her. I sat. "Did you enjoy the concert last night?"

How did she always know? "I wasn't spying on you, honest."

"It's nice when someone worries about you," she said. "I hadn't played like that in years. It was a flash of brilliance, a swan song perhaps, for it may never happen again. So I took advantage of my returned talent and played every funeral march I knew. Believe me, there were a lot of them."

"I noticed."

"Did you hear the Beethoven sonata? The *Appas-*

*sionata?* It was his best and I remembered all of it."
She looked at her crooked fingers, turning them over
in front of her.

"Your playing was fantastic." I tried to keep her
spirits up. "Just like on the tape." Tomcat jumped in
my lap and settled into a ball.

"Too bad I'll never play it again."

"Why not?" Tomcat rolled over onto his back and I
rubbed his belly.

"Well, it was thrilling to feel the power in my hands
once more, but it took me too much into the past. I
imagined I was young again, sitting at my beautiful
Steinway D, speaking to an audience through the
music, playing out my mood and emotions, and
Beethoven's, too. I felt it so strongly when I was
finished, I was surprised there wasn't any applause."
Fern was silent for a moment, rubbing one hand
against the other. "It's not good to live in the past.
Those days can never be again."

"Don't say that," I said. "You'll have some more
good days."

Lifting my hand away from Tomcat, she looked in
my eyes. "The good days are all gone, Veronica." The
words sent a chill through me, right down to my
flip-flops. "But not for you. Your good times are just
beginning. If you work hard, you may even major in
music in college." I felt her turn my hand over and

stroke it. "You probably won't be a concert pianist, but a music teacher, maybe."

"A piano teacher?" I tried to imagine myself pounding kids on the back and demanding that they count louder. "Why not a concert artist?"

"You have a wonderful talent for music that will take you far, and if you want to be a concert artist, you might make it happen. But you will always be just very good. You are not like me. You are not a genius." She was emphatic.

I felt angry, and disappointed. Who was she, an eccentric, old catlady, to tell me I wasn't a genius?

"Remember what I told you before, Veronica? That it's better to be well-rounded than unbalanced? There will be many good things in your life," she predicted, "and the piano will be one of them."

I immediately felt guilty for thinking of her as an old catlady. Maybe she was right and I wasn't a genius. But her words certainly made me more determined than ever to learn to play well. I wondered what the other good things in my future would be.

"Oh, I almost forgot something." Fern went to her bedroom and came back with a polished wooden box. The top was decorated with tiny flowers made up of small pieces of colored wood. She held it out to me. "Open it."

Putting Tomcat on the sofa next to me, I raised the

lid. From the box came the melody of the *Moonlight* Sonata.

"It's beautiful," I said.

"I won this music box in a Beethoven contest when I was ten years old. It was first prize, and now it's for you."

"For me? Oh, I couldn't take it."

"You have to take it, Veronica. It's your wedding present." I thought Fern was kidding.

"My wedding present? I'm not getting married!"

"I'm thinking of someday in the future, when you will be old enough. And since I won't be here to come to the wedding, I'm giving it to you early."

"But . . ."

"Now what's the matter?" she asked.

"What if I never get married?"

"I'm betting that you will, but if not, it can be a graduation from high school present, or a birthday present some year when everyone else forgets. If you ever do become a piano teacher, give it to that special student. The one who makes your teaching worthwhile."

I closed the lid, and the music stopped. At the same time, the phone in the kitchen rang. I watched Fern pull a large hairpin from one side of her head, which made half of her frizzy hair stand straight out. She carefully smoothed it back and replaced the pin.

"Aren't you going to answer the phone?"

"There's nobody I want to talk to," she said, rearranging the pin from the other side, in the same way. The phone kept ringing.

"What if it's important?"

"Okay, okay, Veronica. But it's always bad news." She walked to the kitchen and slowly picked up the receiver.

"Hello. Well, what do you want?" Fern's voice was gruff, and increasingly upset. "You're *what?*" I watched her eyebrows bob up and down. "Stay away. You're not welcome here." Slamming down the receiver, she stumbled back into the living room and plopped down on the sofa.

"What's wrong?"

"It's George. He's coming to see me tomorrow." Her eyes glistened as she leaned close to me and whispered. "And he's bringing something to show me— says it has to do with that old people's home. Maybe they're legal papers. Veronica, I think he's going to put me away."

"Maybe he just wants to talk, like last time." I didn't want Fern to move away. No one could teach the piano like her, and since the Clamdiggers had fallen apart, she was my best friend.

"No, Veronica. This time I think George means business." Fern patted her lap and Uncle Newt climbed in. With her yellowed nails, she scratched the cat's white fur. "George is not a bad boy. He just thinks I can't take care of myself anymore." She paused and looked across the room to the mess in the kitchen. "In short, he's afraid I'll drop dead one day, all alone in this house."

I thought about Fern's dizzy spells, the way she smelled, and the filthy kitchen. Eighty-three was very old. Could Mr. Peet be right? Maybe she needed to be in a home where she could be looked after.

"But Veronica." Fern grabbed my hand and held it tight. "George doesn't understand that there are things worse than death. I'm not afraid to die. But giving up my family, never visiting the green heron or my sacred woods—that I'm afraid of. That is a fate far worse than death itself."

I thought of the woods, the way they smelled of pine after a rain, the way the sun's rays split through the trees, the way the squirrels rustled the leaves as they played. Couldn't she stay in her old house just awhile longer? There had to be a way.

# 18

# Clamdiggers to the Rescue

*I was on my way home from Fern's when the* answer came to me. I had been thinking about the piles of crusty dishes in the sink, the layers of dirt on the kitchen floor, the yard that only got cut once or twice a year when Smitty couldn't stand it any longer. If only her place looked nice, then maybe George would believe that Fern could manage on her own. That was it!

Of course, I would need lots of help to make everything neat in one day, I thought. That meant Jimmy and Amy would have to agree to pitch in. Then there was the question of how Fern would take it. She seemed to like her house just the way it was. "First things first," I said to myself, running inside to put my music box away and to call Amy.

She agreed to meet me at Hadley's, where Jimmy was working until noon. I didn't tell her what I wanted, just that we had to have an emergency meeting of the Clamdiggers.

When I arrived at the marina, Jimmy was kneeling on the upside-down bottom of a boat, and Amy was admiring his work.

"This had better be important," she said to me. "I just polished my nails and I had to come running over here before they were even dry."

"What's up, Ronnie?" Jimmy asked. Still holding the sanding block, he lifted the hair off his sweaty forehead with the back of his hand.

"Fern's son is coming to see her tomorrow," I explained. "We're almost certain he wants to move her to an old people's home in Lansing because he thinks she can't take care of herself."

"What could this possibly have to do with us?" Amy pouted.

"Fern doesn't want to go," I explained patiently. "She says she'd rather die than be taken away from Harbor Island and her cats." I glanced up at Jimmy who was sitting on his heels, hands on the knees of his holey jeans, then over at Amy, who was watching me suspiciously. "We've got to make everything look so good that he'll see he's wrong and let her stay. I want you two to help me clean up her place." I rushed the final words.

"You want *me* to help you clean Mrs. Peet's house?" Amy's response wasn't exactly enthusiastic.

"Yes, and we have to do the whole job today," I said, trying to make it sound like she had no choice.

"I'll help," Jimmy offered. "When I get off at twelve, I'll come over and take care of the yard."

"What about you, Amy?" I stared directly into her wide violet eyes.

"No thanks. Old lady Peet probably does belong in a home somewhere. And even if we did clean the house, she'd still look the same . . . and smell the same!" Amy pinched her nose between two silver nailtips.

That was something I hadn't thought of. Even if we did make everything spotless, there was still the problem of how Fern looked. It would take some transformation to turn her into somebody's grandma overnight. Of course, who else?

"You could do it, Amy," I gushed. "You love doing hair and this would be a real challenge. I'll clean up the house, Jimmy can fix up the yard, and *you* can fix up Fern!"

Amy screwed up her face and curled her upper lip. "Are you out of your mind, Ronnie? It gives me goose bumps to even think of touching her hair. Who knows what's living in it?"

"What if I got her to wash it first? And you could wear gloves and give her a perm. That smelly stuff would kill anything."

"You want me to use my rods and perm kit I just bought with my own money on Mrs. Peet?" She looked up at Jimmy, then back at me, shook her head, and went straight to the point: "Yuck!"

"I wouldn't want to mess around with that hair, either," Jimmy said. "But if anyone can do it, you can, Aim."

Oh great, I thought, now he's got a pet name for her. Amy ducked her head and rolled her eyes up at Jimmy. He answered by flashing her that crooked smile.

"But . . . that hair. It's such a rat's nest," she argued.

Jimmy hopped off the boat bottom and threw his arm around my shoulders. "Ronnie and I really need your help, Aim. Remember, Clamdiggers forever!"

I think his arm around me was the last straw because Amy gave a little shiver and said, "Promise you'll get her to wash it first?"

"I promise." But I didn't have the slightest idea how I was going to do it. "Meet me at Fern's house with all your stuff."

"Great!" Jimmy exclaimed, dropping his arm. "I'll go see Mr. Hadley about borrowing his riding mower."

"So much for the waterskiing." Amy sighed.

*        *        *

A short half hour later I was walking down Beach Road with a bucket full of Mom's cleaning supplies.

"What's all this, Veronica?" Fern asked, greeting me at her door.

"Just some cleaning stuff," I replied casually. "I thought I'd dust and straighten up a little." I set the bucket on the counter next to Fern's sink and started washing the dishes with my sponge but it wasn't enough. So I reached for a soap pad and scrubbed hard at the bits of dried fish stew. Some began to flake off.

"Don't be silly, Veronica," Fern scolded. "I don't expect you to do my dishes. Besides, they're clean enough for my family the way they are."

"Mr. Peet doesn't think so," I said. "I'm going to make the place look so good that when he comes tomorrow, he'll forget about making you move to Lansing."

"Oh, so that's it." Fern sat at her table and rested her chin on her hands. Both bobby pins were lost now, making her hair fuzz out all around her face. "It won't do any good. When George makes up his mind about something, he's not likely to change it."

I rinsed the plates and stacked them on a clean dish towel I'd brought from home. An engine roared in the driveway.

"What's all that racket outside?" Fern asked,

peering out the window. "Why, it's Jimmy. He's riding around my yard on a tractor!"

"He's cutting the grass," I explained. There was an iron skillet at the bottom of the sink that had sat there so long it had rusted. I scrubbed it with the soap pad, rinsed, and dried it.

"Oh no, Veronica," Fern protested, grabbing at the dish towel. "You shouldn't be doing this." When I didn't let go of the other end, her eyes squinted and her mouth formed a thin, tight line. "You're just like George—you think I can't take care of myself."

"You could use a little help, that's all."

"I never took charity in my whole life, and I'm not about to start now."

"It's not charity, Fern," I said politely. "Friends are supposed to help each other." I gave a quick tug on the towel and it slipped out of her hands. "Just like you giving me piano lessons for free. Now it's your turn."

Gradually her eyes opened wide and the tight line of her mouth relaxed. "I never had many friends," she said. "My music took most of my time."

By now, I'd reached the bottom of the sink. It was covered with thick, brown slime. I took a big breath and scrubbed hard. Slowly, white patches appeared. Suddenly the screen door banged.

"Well, well," Fern said, eyeing Amy and the blow

146

dryer that stuck out of her bag. "I'm afraid to ask what your job is."

Amy took one look at Fern's hair and backed up a step.

"Amy wants to be a beautician when she grows up," I ad-libbed, "and she needs someone to practice on."

"I don't want to be a—" Amy began, but Fern interrupted.

"My hair?" She grabbed a stray piece and examined it. "Veronica, you've gone too far! I've worn my hair this way for years, and it suits me perfectly. If I changed it, my family wouldn't recognize me."

"Well, in that case, maybe I should leave," Amy said. I could see my plan going down the drain with the brown slime.

"No! Wait, Amy." Turning to Fern, I said, "I know you don't like all these changes, but think what will happen if your son moves you into that home. Then *everything* will change. And think about your cats. What will they do without you?" Fern sat heavily in her chair and stared at me. Her expression reminded me of a little kid, pouting. "Please Fern," I begged. "I don't know if it will help, but we *have* to try."

She sat quietly for a minute. "Do you think it will work?" she asked, looking over at Amy, then back at me. "I'd rather die than go to the retirement home."

"Let me help you wash your hair first," Amy said

gently. "We can pull a chair up to the sink and it will be just like a beauty shop." She smiled at Fern, and I knew why I still liked Amy, even after all the trouble she'd caused.

"I haven't been to the beauty parlor in a long time," Fern said wistfully.

So we got started. Fern was so short that we had to stack several inches of newspapers on the chair. While Amy put on her gloves, I put the dishes away. It made a dent in the clutter, but the counter was still loaded with foil, plastic bread bags, old shoe laces, rubber bands, and tons of other junk.

With spray cleaner and a rag, I wiped a layer of greasy cat hair off the fridge and stove. The hairs turned my rag gray. Then I sorted through all the junk on the counter.

"Don't go throwing anything out," Fern said. "It took me a long time to save those things." I thought her voice sounded funny, maybe because her head was back over the sink. Gingerly, Amy was running water through her hair.

"How about if I put everything in the cupboards somewhere?" I asked.

"I guess that would be okay," Fern agreed. "Ouch! This old neck doesn't bend like it used to, young lady."

"Sorry," Amy said.

I made neat stacks of folded grocery bags and foil pieces. When I found the big ball of string, with the metal end of my fish stringer still sticking out of it, I put it in a cabinet with the rest of the stuff.

"Aaahhh!" Amy screamed, and suds flew everywhere. Tomcat stood on the counter, hissing and spitting at her.

"What's going on?" Fern asked. "I can't see a thing with all this soap in my face."

"Don't be afraid, Amy," I said. "It's only Tomcat." Talking softly, I stroked him until his fur went down. Then I scooped the cat up in my arms. "Where did he come from?"

Amy pointed to the row of ceramic canisters next to the sink. "He was hiding behind there. I reached for the shampoo and got the end of his tail instead."

"You probably scared him." I giggled.

Amy leaned close to my ear and whispered, "Get him out of here or I quit!"

"Young lady, could you please get the soap off my face?" Fern pleaded.

I left to clean the bathroom, taking Tomcat with me. I had never been in the bathroom before—it was a disaster like everywhere else. The white finish on the sink was scratched, there were big rust stains in the toilet bowl, and today Uncle Newt and Aunt Hester were curled up in the tub. It took me an hour to scrub all the dirt out of the cracks between the ceramic tiles, especially with three cats rubbing up against me, but when I finished, everything sparkled.

By the time I got back to the kitchen, the clock said it was almost three, and Amy had unrolled Fern's hair and was blowing it dry. Long, kinky curls of gray and yellowish white danced in the air from the hot dryer. If Fern looked eccentric before, she was a wild woman now.

"Maybe I should have used bigger rods," Amy whispered hesitantly. "Or cut it first."

"Well, how did it turn out?" Fern asked. "Can I see it now?"

I didn't want Fern to know how strange she looked. I was sure if she saw herself in the mirror, she'd probably kick us all out.

"I still need to cut it," Amy told her, grabbing a scissors and whacking off a big piece. I pulled up a chair and watched as loops of hair fell to the floor. Soon Fern's head was a big, curly ball, a dubious improvement.

"Are you done *yet*?" Fern asked.

"No," I answered quickly. "Amy still has to do something else. Don't you, Amy?"

Amy shrugged her shoulders. "I could trim it back over the ears and wash it again. Maybe it needs to relax a little." I prayed it would relax a lot.

This time when Amy finished, the curls were a lot

softer and lay close to Fern's head. The style wasn't terrific, but her hair was clean, and the wild look was gone. Amy and I exchanged worried glances when Fern went to inspect herself in the bathroom.

"My, my!" she said, emerging with a smile. "That bathroom is as clean as a whistle!" She patted her head with her hand, and twisted the curls around her fingers. "And my hair . . . it's so . . . oh dear . . ." She took a step forward and began to wobble. "I think I'd better lie down. All this excitement is making me tired."

Amy and I helped Fern to the sofa, where she lay down with her head on a pillow.

"Are you dizzy again?" I asked.

"No, I'm just tired. I usually take little cat naps in the afternoon, just like Fatcat. I think I'll take a short one now, while you girls finish your work."

Amy and I went to the kitchen to tackle the floor.

"Do you think she liked her hair?" Amy asked when we were both on hands and knees, scrubbing through years of grimy wax.

"I don't know. With Fern it's hard to tell."

I was surprised at how much Amy was being a good sport about things. She scrubbed the floor so hard, she wore through the plastic gloves and had to throw them away. Her silver nail polish was ruined, but she didn't seem to notice. She even shooed Tomcat out of her way several times without screaming at him. The ultimate was the pile of cat poop she found in the corner by the fridge. I watched her gag twice, roll it up in newspaper, and go on cleaning. We were still working when Jimmy shouted through the screen that the grass was cut, and the outside of the windows were washed.

"I've got to get the mower back to the marina." He waved. "See ya later."

"Yeah, later," Amy called.

After we finished the floor, we were surprised to find it was light sky blue with little colored specks in it. Then we cleaned the bedroom, too, and quietly dusted the living room. Fern woke up just as we were putting our stuff away.

"You have both worked so hard. Thank you so much for your help," she said sleepily. "And be sure and thank Jimmy, too."

"We will," I assured her.

"Veronica, would you get a catfish from the freezer and set it out to defrost? I think I'll stay right here on the couch for a while." She pulled the afghan from the back of the sofa, and covered herself up.

I left the catfish, wrapped in white paper, on the counter by the sink. While Amy and I gathered up our things, I looked around. There was still lots left undone, but everything looked clean and smelled like Lysol, instead of cat. I was proud of myself and Amy too. "Mr. Peet will certainly be impressed tomorrow," I said.

"You girls run along now," Fern called from the living room. "And Veronica, come by in the morning for your lesson."

"I'll be here. Good-bye, Fern."

As we walked out the door, she yelled after us, "You did a fine job on my hair, Amy. You'll make a wonderful beautician someday."

Amy and I stopped in the road to study the house. It needed a coat of paint, but Jimmy's job on the yard was a huge improvement. He had even weeded the small garden by the front door and trimmed the two nearby shrubs into neat round balls.

"Thanks for your help, Amy," I said. "I couldn't have done it without you, and her hair turned out terrific."

"I was a little worried there for a while," she confessed.

"Me, too. I'll never forget those long kinky curls flying every which way, and you hacking them off, right and left with the scissors. Or that cat poop. You wrapped it so neatly!"

"Yeah, that's me," she said. "The best cat poop-wrapper in all of Michigan!" We both giggled. It was just like having the old Amy back again, and I felt the closest to her I had all summer.

Then she switched gears. "I split my longest nail," she said, holding her finger up. "I've got to get home and fix it right away. And Ronnie—I know she's your friend and all, but I think she'd be better off in a home. Especially with those dizzy spells." She walked down the road, still examining her split nail. I guess the old Amy never really left, she just got mixed in with the new one somehow, and maybe it wasn't such a bad combination.

# 19

# Fern's Escape

*That night, I was dead tired from all that* housework. I took a bath right after supper and was fast asleep by eight-thirty. Mom woke me up once to see if I was sick, but after feeling my forehead, she decided I was okay.

The next morning I was wide awake at six, wondering when Mr. Peet would show up at Fern's. Too restless to stay in bed, I left Mom and Dad a note and, taking my pole and minnow bucket, went to the bridge to fish. Amy's curtains were closed when I passed by.

Leaving my pole and bait on the wooden bridge, I walked across it to Hadley's. The Quonsets were locked with chains and padlocks, and two mourning doves cooed at me from the top of the vending shack. After searching my pockets for change, I bought a can of pop and a Milky Way for breakfast. Heading back toward my gear, I saw Boogie standing on the bridge with his head buried in the minnow bucket, his tail wagging in circles.

"Boogie! *No!*" I yelled, breaking into a run. Since I was still mad at him over Toothless, I was ready to smack him a good one for stealing my bait. Just as I raced up behind him he threw his head up in the air. I could see a tiny minnow tail flipping back and forth as it slid into his mouth. In one gulp, it was gone. Then Boogie gave me such a sheepish look that I couldn't bring myself to hit him. "What a ridiculous dog you are," I said, scratching him on the rump instead. I didn't even get mad when I saw that he had drunk most of the water and left only two minnows. Oh well, I thought. They would last me for a little while.

Sitting on the bridge railing, my line in the water below, I finished my candy bar and watched the boats bobbing in their slips along the narrow channel that separated Harbor Island from the mainland.

The bridge shook and rumbled as Mr. Jackman drove across and waved. Then Mrs. Parrish walked by and said hello before setting up her easel on the channel bank. By the time Mr. Hadley opened the marina, I had caught a crappie and a small perch. They would be enough for the cats' supper, I thought, packing up to go to Fern's. As I retraced my path on Beach Road, I saw the Kowalski twins coming my way.

"Where are you going all by yourselves?" I asked.

"Just to Hadley's to buy milk for Mom," Jessie said. It was then that I noticed they each had on a decaying clam shell necklace.

"Hey! Where did you get those?" I guess I didn't sound too friendly because they both fingered the shells and ran off.

Arriving at Fern's, I went around to her back step and called through the open kitchen door. "Fern, it's Veronica. Can I come in?" Tomcat came to the door, put his front paws on the screen, stretched, and meowed.

"Hi fella. Where's Fern?" He hunched his back and purred.

Cautiously, I went inside. Tomcat stood on tiptoe to sniff the fish hanging from my stringer. I smelled fish, too—old, spoiled, rotting fish. Then I saw Uncle Newt, Blackcat, Birdy, and Fatcat sitting on the counter nibbling on a raw catfish. They had chewed their way through the freezer paper it was wrapped in.

"Whew!" I said, shooing them away. That catfish was lying exactly where I'd left it the night before. I picked it up and dropped it in the garbage.

"Fern, Fern! Where are you?" I shouted. Looking across the kitchen table into the living room, I could see her, lying on the sofa. Taking one step into the room, I called, "Fern, wake up, Fern." She didn't move. "Fern, *Fern!*" This time I yelled as loud as I could, but I knew it wouldn't do any good, and I was afraid to go any closer.

"Mom, Mom! You've got to do something quick!" I was out of breath from running home. Luckily Mom hadn't left for work yet and was there, fixing her hair.

"What's the matter, Ronnie?" she asked, brush in hand.

"It's Fern. Something's wrong—she's just lying there on the sofa and won't move. I think maybe she's, she's . . ."

"She's what?" Mom asked.

"I don't know, but you've got to do something quick!"

She went to the phone and called the Northwood fire department, asked them to send an ambulance, and gave them Fern's address. "Come on, Ronnie," she said as she hung up.

Mom didn't bother with the car. She ran the short distance down the road toward Fern's. Running beside her, I was amazed by her speed. When Mom opened Fern's back door, several cats jumped out of the way.

"Wait here," she insisted, and went into the living room. I bent down to pet the cats and I could hear Mom calling softly to my friend. Then she came back into the kitchen. "Ronnie, let's go outside."

I followed her out the front door, and we sat down on the porch step. Mom put her arms around me and said, "Ronnie, she's dead."

I heard the sirens soft and far away at first. I guessed they came from the highway. Then they changed direction and got louder. The bridge rumbled and a few seconds later a greenish yellow ambulance with red crosses painted on the doors slid into Fern's driveway. Two men in white jumped out.

"Inside, on the living room couch," Mom said as we stood up to let them pass.

Mom's wrong, I thought. Fern must have fainted or something. Yes, that was it—another dizzy spell. They'd see—the paramedics—they'd tell Mom she was wrong.

"Are you a relative?" one of the men asked Mom, stepping back outside.

"No, Mrs. Peet is my daughter's piano teacher," she explained.

"She fainted, didn't she?" I wasn't sure I wanted an answer to my question.

"I'm sorry," he said, shaking his head. "There's nothing we can do. She's been dead for several hours—probably died sometime during the night. Looks like she had a stroke."

The man had on a white jacket, white pants, and white shoes. A black stethoscope hung around his neck. I walked away and sat on the grass under the oak tree—the one Toothless had climbed to escape Boogie.

Amy and Jimmy came down the road, pumping hard on their bikes. They coasted across the grass and stopped in front of me.

"What happened, Ronnie?" Jimmy asked. "Is Mrs. Peet okay?"

"No," I answered. "She's not and never will be again."

"You mean . . . she's dead?" Amy asked. I nodded.

We watched as the paramedics came out of the house carrying a narrow stretcher between them. They stopped, lowered the wheels, and pushed it to the ambulance. We couldn't see Fern, just a body. A very small body, wrapped in a blanket. Abruptly, the wheels swung up, out of the way, and the two men pushed the cart into the back of the ambulance. They stood talking to Mom for a minute or so, then she turned and signaled to me. Amy and Jimmy laid their bikes in the grass, and we walked over to her together.

"Do you know if Mrs. Peet has any relatives we can call?" one of the men asked.

"Just her son, Mr. George Peet, from Lansing," I replied. "Fern said he was coming for a visit later today."

"Okay, thanks," he said. "We'll have the police get in touch with him right away."

"What are you going to do with Fern?" I asked.

"We'll take her to the Northwood morgue until her son comes for her. Can you people take care of the house and all those cats until Mr. Peet gets here?"

"I'll take care of everything," I said.

As the ambulance pulled away, Mom said, "Let's look inside for a key, so we can lock the house and go home."

"She keeps it on top of the piano," I told her.

"I'll get it." Jimmy hurried inside. When he was locking the door, I remembered the cats nibbling on the spoiled fish.

"Wait a minute," I said. "The cats are hungry. They didn't get anything to eat last night."

"You can come back later." Mom gently pushed me forward. "I think we all need to go home now."

As we headed for the road, Amy hugged me and whispered in my ear, "I'm sorry Ronnie. I know she was your friend."

"Me, too," Jimmy added. "It's hard to believe she's dead."

"Yeah, especially when just yesterday . . ." Amy's voice trailed off and she scuffed her feet in the grass.

"At least we tried," I said, remembering. "We gave her the cleanest house she'd had in years."

Mom put her arm around me and we walked home together. Fern had been right when she'd said her good days were over. Now she was gone. I would have cried if I hadn't felt numb all over.

# 20

# A Steinway of My Own

*The rest of that day was awful. Mom tried to* get me to eat lunch, but my stomach was tied up in knots. So we sat at the kitchen table and had a long talk about Fern. I described Mr. Peet's threat to put Fern in a retirement home, and how Jimmy and Amy and I cleaned the house.

"I had no idea things were that bad," Mom said. "Maybe Mr. Peet was right to try to move his mother to Lansing."

"But Mom, he didn't understand Fern. She told me she'd rather be dead than live in a home somewhere where she couldn't have her cats, or visit the woods. Doesn't that count for something?"

"It should, but it doesn't always. When people can't take care of themselves anymore, sometimes they have to give up living alone, even if they don't want to."

I supposed she was right—after all, my mom's pretty smart—but I knew Fern wouldn't have agreed.

Mom shook her head and chuckled. "I was just imagining the three of you cleaning that house."

"That was nothing. You should have seen Amy giving Fern a perm."

"Amy gave Mrs. Peet a perm?"

"Yeah, she wore gloves and everything. She shampooed Fern's hair three times because she was afraid of lice." Mom smiled. Thinking about it made me smile, too.

"She certainly was an interesting person," Mom said after a while, "and I know you will miss her."

"There's one more thing, Mom." I wanted to let go of all my secrets. "Fern's husband left her a lot of money, and she spent most of it on something years ago. She was so poor she had to sell one of her pianos. Now I'll never know what she spent all her money on." It felt good to be able to tell Mom everything at last.

I traced one of the flowers on the vinyl tablecloth with my finger. Two tears hit separate petals, and I wiped them away with my hand. Then I put my head down on the table and cried until the knots in my stomach came untangled.

When it was over, I felt very sleepy. Mom gave me

a hug and sent me to bed. The next thing I knew, it was six-thirty at night.

All I could manage for dinner was a small dish of applesauce, but Mom and Dad didn't complain. I had to explain everything all over again to Dad. I waited until Mom cleared the table, then I brought out my music box and notebook.

"It's beautiful," Mom said, running her fingers over the glossy lid of the box. "How nice of her to give it to you."

Dad turned the pages of my notebook. "These pieces are very special, too," he said. "Original compositions by a great artist, and dedicated to you. 'Tomcat Boogie,' " he read. "I'd like to hear that one."

I thought of Tomcat walking over the keys the day of my first lesson, and remembered the family. "Can I take some food to the cats now? They must be very hungry, and I don't know if Mr. Peet ever came today or not." Mom glanced at Dad and nodded.

I filled a big mixing bowl with leftovers from the fridge and dumped a couple of cans of tuna on top.

"I'm going with you," Dad said, getting up from his chair.

"Please, I want to go by myself."

"You sure?" Mom asked.

"Yes." I grabbed the key and left.

The Woods Brothers were sitting on the porch step when I got to Fern's. As soon as I opened the door, they darted inside, avoiding getting close to me. But Tomcat came up and rubbed against my legs.

"Here kitty, kitty, kitty, come and get your supper," I called, putting the bowl of food on the floor. Cats came from everywhere. Birdy jumped from the top of the fridge to the counter and hissed at Aunt Hester. Cousin Jake tried to bite Brother Blackie. One of the Woods Brothers jumped in the bowl and a full-scale war broke out. The growling, hissing, and howling had me convinced they were going to tear each other to shreds.

"Stop it! Stop it right now!" I grabbed two skillets and banged them together. Cats scattered. Soon I was alone in the kitchen.

I remembered Fern saying her family was a wild bunch and didn't like changes in routine. Thinking about that gave me an idea. I set the table with dinner plates and divided up the food just like Fern always did.

"Here, children. Here's your supper," I called. Tomcat was the first to appear, and I picked him up and set him on the table. He sniffed the food, then nibbled on the tuna. One by one, the others joined him, until they were all in their proper places.

Leaving them to eat, I went into the living room, sat at the piano, and played a few scales. If only I were good enough to play Chopin's funeral march for Fern, I thought. But I knew it would take years of practice

165

before I could manage something like that. Instead I played the "Waltz of the Green Heron." I was almost done when I heard the front door open and a man's voice speaking to me.

"That was very good. Mother would be quite proud." Mr. Peet walked over to the couch and sat down.

"I came to feed the cats," I explained. "I promised the paramedics I'd look after them until you could take care of things."

"Thanks for your help." He glanced around the room. "The house sure looks different. When I drove up, I noticed the lawn had been cut, and everything in here is clean, too." He peered at me intently. "Are you responsible for all this?"

"My friends helped me. We thought if we fixed things up, you'd let Fern stay awhile longer." Tomcat hopped in my lap and sat there, washing his face with his paw.

"You did a nice job on the house," he repeated, a bit embarrassed. "I'm glad Mother had such a good friend." He settled back on the couch.

"Fern said you were bringing papers for her to sign. She thought you were going to put her away in an old folks' home."

"Well," he began, taking out his handkerchief and wiping a trickle of sweat from his forehead. "I was thinking about it, but the papers I was bringing today were some color brochures on Maple Hills Retirement

Center. The last time I was here it was clear that Mother couldn't go on living alone any longer—she wasn't taking care of herself. So I put her name on a waiting list at the home. They called last week to tell me they had a room for her. I wanted one last try to convince her to move. If she refused, well, then I was prepared to force her."

"But what about what Fern wanted?" I asked him. "She always said she wasn't afraid to die as long as she could go right here in this house with her family. Don't old people have the right to choose where they want to live . . . and die?" Tomcat rubbed his head against my arm and began to purr.

Mr. Peet crossed his legs and said, "But she was my mother—I was responsible for her—I didn't want her to die. I let her stay here far too long," he explained. "If I'd gotten her out of here sooner, and had the doctor at Maple Hills check her over, maybe her stroke could have been prevented. I'll have to live with the guilt over that a long time." His voice trembled and he patted his neck with the handkerchief.

"It wasn't your fault she died," I said, feeling sorry for him. I suppose I could understand Mr. Peet's reasons for wanting to put his mother in a home, but I was glad Fern would never have to live there. "When is the funeral?"

"There isn't any," Mr. Peet answered. "I'm having

Mother cremated and the ashes sent back to Lansing for burial. She didn't have too many close friends here, so a simple memorial service at the cemetery seems best." He folded his handkerchief and tucked it in his shirt pocket. Then he stood up and came over to the piano, resting his hand on the top.

"I'm glad you were here when I came in, Veronica. It makes it easy for me to tell you that I want you to have the piano. There's no place for it at my house."

"You're giving me the piano? But I couldn't—I mean, it's such an expensive gift."

Mr. Peet shook his head, as if to stop my objections. "Please take it, Veronica. I'm sure Mother would have wanted it that way, and so do I."

Fern's Steinway practice piano—my piano! "Thank you, Mr. Peet," I said. Thank you, thank you, *thank you*, Fern, I thought. I pictured it in my living room. We could move the couch over and make a place for it in the corner. Just wait till Mom and Dad found out! "I'll think of her every time I play it," I told Mr. Peet as I ran my hand over the piano's black, crackled paint.

"There's one other thing I think you'd like to know," he said. "Back in June, Mother told me she had spent all her money. I found that hard to believe, so I went in to the Northwood Bank and Trust and talked to Mike Larkins. He said he couldn't give out information on accounts, but my mother had closed all hers years ago, except for a checking account. And even that had run out a while back. Imagine how shocked I was to find out her inheritance was really gone. Then Mike hinted that maybe I would like to visit the courthouse while I was in town. So I did just that, and found out Mother owned a lot of land."

"Land?" I had wondered all summer where Fern's money had gone.

"Right after Dad died, Mother wanted to get away from the city, so she moved here, to this small cottage. Shortly after that the rest of the island came up for development and she bought it—all of it."

"You mean Fern owned all the vacant lots, and the woods, and the cove, and the bog, and—"

"The whole thing," he interrupted. "I talked to her attorney this morning, right after I took care of the arrangements for the ashes. He told me Mother left it all to the Harbor Island Homeowners group to manage. They are allowed to sell the ten lots on this side and use that money for a fund to maintain the rest as a wildlife refuge." Fatcat ambled over to the piano and made a leap for the top. He missed and landed on the keys with a crashing chord.

So reminded, I asked, "What are you going to do about the cats?"

"Well . . . I can't very well keep them now, can I? And homes for grown cats are hard to find." George hesitated and I watched the perspiration glisten on his bald spot. "I'll just have to put them to sleep. I've got some cages out in the car that the Northwood veterinary clinic loaned me this afternoon. I decided I couldn't very well just leave all those cats shut up in here to starve while I make arrangements to sell the house. Although my mom was very good with animals, I'm not. Would you help me get them in the cages?" He looked at me with watery blue eyes, just like Fern's.

"How can you put them to sleep? Fern loved her cats—they were her family!" I squeezed Tomcat so hard he squirmed.

"I don't like doing it." George's voice was apologetic. "Would you like to have any of them?"

I looked over at the table where most of the family still sat—some were washing themselves and some were licking their plates clean. Uncle Newt was almost blind, and wouldn't move without Aunt Hester. Brother Blackie and Cousin Jake raided garbage cans and fought constantly. Birdy would bite if touched, and Fatcat slept in the road all day. Only Tomcat would make a good pet. The rest would have to go with Mr. Peet.

"I'm keeping Tomcat," I said. "And you can let the Woods Brothers go. They're wild anyway." I shoved Tomcat on top of the piano. "I'll help you with the rest."

The cats were easy to catch, except for Birdy, who

led us on a chase all over the house. We finally cornered her under Fern's dresser. "Grrrrr," she growled at me when I put my hand out to her.

"Here, let's try this," Mr. Peet suggested. He threw a bath towel over her, grabbed, and missed. Birdy came out from under the dresser howling, the towel still on top of her. Mr. Peet pulled the quilt off the bed and threw it on top of the towel. We both grabbed the ends and rolled Birdy into a ball. I ran outside and stuffed the whole thing into a cage. It only took her a few seconds to rip her way out.

"Wow! What a devil that one is," Mr. Peet said.

"Yeah," I agreed. "She doesn't like to be touched."

What was left of Fern's family sat huddled in the little wire cages in Mr. Peet's car. Fatcat scratched at the corner of his and meowed. I took one last look, and hugging Tomcat close, walked home.

# Good-bye Amy

*A week after Fern's death, Mr. Peet came* back to start cleaning out the cottage. Dad, Jimmy, and Smitty all went over there with me, and we moved the piano to my house on the back of Smitty's carpenter truck. As soon as we had it in place in the corner of my living room, Tomcat launched himself to the top and paced back and forth. Mom folded an old blanket and laid it on the piano. Tomcat immediately lay down on it and began to purr. I was so thrilled to have Fern's piano that I practiced almost three hours that first day.

The rest of August went by fast. Jimmy, Amy, and I skied as often as we could, although I never did try it barefoot again, and Amy paid strict attention when she spotted me.

Fern's cottage was sold to a retired couple who put up cream-colored aluminum siding and painted the trim brown. The cement statue cats disappeared, and the house looked so different it was hard to believe that Fern had ever lived there.


The last day of Labor Day weekend, the Clamdiggers met for a picnic in the woods beyond the bog.

"I wish you didn't have to go back to Detroit today, Aim," Jimmy said. We were all sitting Indian-style on an old plastic tablecloth, a few yards from the row of catnip-covered graves.

"Me, too," she said. "Summer went by fast this year."

"It goes by fast every year," I said. It was hot and still in the the sacred woods. Reaching over the tablecloth, I picked up a handful of dead pine needles and let them slide through my fingers. "But the woods will be here anytime we want, thanks to Fern."

"As long as I live, I'll never forget that cat funeral," Jimmy said.

"Yeah, that was one wild scene—Mrs. Peet marching through the bog in that cocktail dress, carrying her dead cat." Amy rolled her eyes and smiled.

"She loved it here so much. I'm glad she never had to leave," I said.

"Me, too," Jimmy agreed. "My dad said the home-owner's group is going to get a sign made for the bridge. It will say 'Harbor Island and Meinhart Wildlife Refuge.' "

I wondered what Fern would have thought of that, and took a big bite of my bacon and mayonnaise sandwich.

"How can you eat that stuff?" Amy asked. "It's a wonder you don't have a hundred zits on your face."

"No zits, Amy, just freckles," I said, but I felt my face with my hand and put down the rest of the sandwich.

"Just think, in two days I'll be in high school," Amy sighed. "I can hardly wait to wear my new fall clothes. I'm going to try out for varsity cheerleading," she went on. "Those two-toned skirts are so cute. I hope I make it."

"You'll make it, Amy." Of course she would, and all the football players would be running over each other, looking at her two-toned skirt and snug sweater.

"And there's the freshman prom in the spring," she gushed. "Can you see me in a pink formal with yards and yards of lace? No, light blue would be better."

"Send me a picture," Jimmy said.

"I will, and I'll send you one, too, Ronnie."

Who would take me to the Northwood High dance? I wondered. Maybe Jimmy, since Amy wouldn't be around, or maybe someone new.

"You'll write to me, won't you, James?" Amy kept her head down, but rolled her eyes up to meet his.

"Of course I will," he answered, his voice getting deeper. "Every day."

Every day? Oh sure, I thought. He didn't even write his own mother the time he went to boy scout camp. Of course, that was different.

"I'm going to miss you, too, Ronnie," Amy said. She put her arm around me and pulled me close. "Clamdiggers forever!" she shouted, and we all hugged each other.

"Yeah, forever," Jimmy repeated.

"Nothing's forever," I said quietly.

"Well, time to go," Amy said, standing up. "I thought I heard a horn honking, and the car must be packed by now."

She shook out the tablecloth, and I took what was left of the food and put it on a stump for the Woods Brothers to find. The catnip on Toothless's grave was spreading fast. I pulled a couple of weeds that had grown up among the leaves and remembered Fern, in her old brown sweater, standing there in her sacred woods that day I was lost. I will miss her, I thought sadly. But I had Tomcat, and the piano, and the music box—my wedding present. Most of all I had the memories.

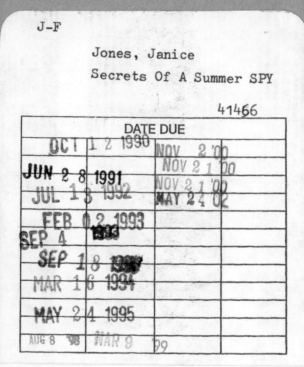